# Arthur

## The Perished Riders MC - Mafia series

## Nicola Jane

Copyright © 2023 by Nicola Jane.

All rights reserved.

No portion of this book may be reproduced in any form without written permission from the publisher or author, except as permitted by U.K. copyright law.

# Meet the Team

Cover Designer: Francessca Wingfield, Wingfield Designs
Editor: Rebecca Vazquez, Dark Syde Books
Proofreader: Jackie Ziegler, Dark Syde Books
Formatting: Nicola Miller

**Spelling Note:**
Please note, this author resides in the United Kingdom and is using British English. Therefore, some words may be viewed as incorrect or spelled incorrectly, however they are not.

**Disclaimer:**

This book is a work of fiction. The names, characters, places, and incidents are all products of the author's imagination and are not to be construed as real. Any similarities are entirely coincidental.

**Note:**
Arthur is the first book in the spin-off series from The Perished Riders MC, where he appears throughout their books as an associate of the club. Therefore, it can be read as a stand-alone.

**Books in The Perished Riders series:**
Maverick: https://mybook.to/Maverick-Perished
Scar: https://mybook.to/Scar-Perished
Grim: https://mybook.to/Grim-Perished
Ghost: https://mybook.to/GhostBk4
Dice: https://mybook.to/DiceBk5

# Social Media

I love to hear from my readers and if you'd like to get in touch, you can find me here . . .

My Website: https://authornicolajane.com/

[My Facebook Page](#)

[My Facebook Readers Group](#)

[Bookbub](#)

[Instagram](#)

[Goodreads](#)

[Amazon](#)

# A word from the Author

THE MATERIAL IN THIS book may be viewed as offensive to some readers, including graphic language, sexual situations, murder, violence, and references to historical sexual assault, although the author does not go into detail.

# Contents

| | |
|---|---|
| Playlist | IX |
| Prologue | 1 |
| Chapter One | 8 |
| Chapter Two | 23 |
| Chapter Three | 37 |
| Chapter Four | 49 |
| Chapter Five | 63 |
| Chapter Six | 77 |
| Chapter Seven | 90 |
| Chapter Eight | 102 |
| Chapter Nine | 119 |
| Chapter Ten | 134 |

| | |
|---|---|
| Chapter Eleven | 149 |
| Chapter Twelve | 163 |
| Chapter Thirteen | 176 |
| Chapter Fourteen | 193 |
| Chapter Fifteen | 206 |
| Chapter Sixteen | 222 |
| Chapter Seventeen | 222 |
| Chapter Eighteen | 222 |
| Chapter Nineteen | 222 |
| Chapter Twenty | 222 |
| Chapter Twenty-One | 222 |
| Epilogue | 222 |
| 1. A Note from me to you | 222 |
| 2. Popular books by Nicola Jane | 222 |

# Playlist

Creep – Kelly Clarkson
Everybody Hurts – Sandra McCracken ft. Liz Vice
Mirrors (Acoustic) – Jonah Baker
You Broke Me First – Conor Maynard
Jolene – Dolly Parton
Blue Skies – Birdy
Wicked Game – Lusaint
Wildfire – Cautious Clay
messy in heaven – venbee & Goddard.
Late Night Talking – Harry Styles
Little Do You Know – Alex & Sierra
Lavender Haze – Taylor Swift

## NICOLA JANE

I Like You (A Happier Song) – Post Malone ft. Doja Cat
2 Be Loved (Am I Ready) – Lizzo
Hide & Seek - Stormzy

# Prologue

ROSEY

I grab the tie belonging to my target. He's attached to it still. He thinks it's a game and willingly follows me through the crowds of people. I did my research and know where all the blind spots are in this place, so I keep my head lowered as we pass under a security camera. I'm pretty sure my dazzling sequined dress will blind any images anyway.

"Fuck, you're so hot," he growls, grabbing my hips and thrusting himself against my behind. I roll my eyes. Does this behaviour actually turn people on? His wandering hands reach around my hips and the heat of his body presses against my back as I continue to lead him to our final destination.

# NICOLA JANE

He doesn't question how I know my way around this nightclub as I lead him up some back stairs. Of course he doesn't, because his end game is different than mine. All he's thinking about is getting his dick sucked. All I'm thinking about is getting the job done so I can go home and get my pyjamas on. Maybe I'll catch Ollie awake. Since he turned ten, he's been trying to push the boundaries and stay up later. I give my head a shake. I can't afford to mess this up because there's big money waiting to be wired into my account.

I push the fire exit door, and we step out onto the roof. This guy's a typical drunk rich boy, hands in my bra, grabbing my tits way too hard to do anything but repulse me. I have yet to find a guy who knows exactly how to touch me to get me going. I manage to get him towards the ledge and I peer over. The streets below are busy and I don't wanna risk him hurting anyone, so I move to the other ledge, making it into a game of chase. I even throw a giggle his way. He falls for of it, desperate for the fuck. Wanker.

I stop, peering over the wall. It's quieter down there, but not so quiet he won't be spotted. His body slams against mine, and the air leaves my lungs. "Fuck, I want you so bad," he growls into my hair, his hands grabbing at my chest again. He's strong for his size, and for a second, I'm transported back

# ARTHUR

to another time. One when I was helpless against the wandering hands and the stale breath near my neck. He yanks my skirt up hard and spins me away from him, bending me over the ledge. This is not how it's meant to go.

"Aren't you married?" I ask as he kicks my legs apart.

"I sleep on the couch," he mutters, taking a fistful of my hair and dragging his wet mouth down my neck.

I'm grossed out. If this was a real hook-up, I'd be so turned off, I'd have to stop it. "Jolene, right?"

I feel him stiffen, and not in the turned-on way. "Huh?"

"Your wife. It's Jolene, right?" He takes an unsteady step back, and I turn to face him, smiling as I lower my dress. "A few pointers . . . not that you'll ever need them again." I take his tie for a second time, and we walk in a circle until his back is to the ledge. "Your hands, way too rough. No woman wants to feel like a slab of meat. And the thrusting . . . oh god, the thrusting . . . I mean, all men do it, right? But why? What makes you think any woman, especially a stranger, wants you to thrust your fucking cock into her back? It's not sexy," I say, throwing my arms in the air, then I place my fingers against my temple.

"Is it like a primal thing? Yah know, *hey, look how big my cock is*? Cos I have to tell you, it's not actually what we think. Just then when you prodded me, my first thought was, gross, obviously. But then I thought about getting home to my own bed and snuggling down to watch Netflix. Is that what you were hoping for when you shoved your erection against me?" He shakes his head slowly, his eyes darting around in panic. "If you really are sleeping on the couch, no wonder. Jolene must be sick of your caveman attitude to sex."

"What's going on?" he asks. "Are you crazy?"

I nod. "A little. It's childhood trauma, apparently. My therapist says I can be fixed, but honestly, I quite like me. Why fix what works? Anyway, back to Jolene. Do you want to know what a woman really wants?" He shrugs, looking around helplessly again. "She wants love, Jeremy. She wants attention. She does not want a cheating husband who thrusts his dick into people's backs, hoping for a quick fuck where I probably wouldn't have even come because, let's face it, Jezza, you're going to be shit in bed, aren't you?"

"I'm sorry, okay. I've never done this before. I don't usually pick up women."

I laugh and it echoes around the rooftop. "I almost feel bad for you. Maybe you weren't loved enough as a kid. Or maybe you settled down too young. You've clearly never been shown how to treat a woman. Now, I could humour your lies, but it's not in my

# ARTHUR

nature. Before you hit the bottom, I want you to think of these people." I open my bag and reveal his iPad. He frowns, not comprehending it's his because he knows he locked it away in the boot of his car. Along with all the dark clothing and the balaclava he uses. It was so cliché.

I begin to scroll through the photos of his victims, photos only he's seen, and the penny begins to drop. He recognises his iPad and his face pales. "You really are a sick fuck. She looks about sixteen. I mean, you've ruined her life forever. Do you think about that when you walk away? Do you consider the damage you've done to a sixteen-year-old virgin? She'll hate men forever. Trust me, I know."

"She . . . she was on . . . I mean, she wanted to meet me."

"Yes, she was on a dating app. But fuck's sake, Jezza, she's sixteen, and you're what, forty? You should know better. You're the adult. And she never joined that app to meet old men who would ruin her life. In her naivety, she thought she'd find a good guy."

"She wanted it rough," he spits.

"No, she didn't. There you go again, reading the room wrong. Does she look happy in this picture, Jeremy?" I thrust the iPad closer, and he turns his head away. The girl in the picture is tied up and sobbing. Her eyes are swollen from tears, and she's covered in bite marks and bruises. "Is that what you were going to do to me tonight?" He shakes his head. "Of course not, because I'm not a kid. I can fight back. You know, Jolene knows what you've done."

His eyes widen in shock. "How?"

"She's very important, or should I say, her family is. Why would you risk it?"

"Did they hire you? Are you here to scare me off, because I'm not leaving my marriage without a pay-out."

I groan. "She said you'd say that."

"You spoke to my wife?"

I put the iPad back in my bag. "The thing is, Jezza," I move closer, "she doesn't want to divorce you."

He looks relieved. "Okay, she wants to work it out. I can stop. I'll stop."

I give him a pitying smile. "Nope. I think she's tired of the shit sex and covering your arse with her brothers." I grimace. "They really don't like you, do they?"

He visibly swallows. "I don't understand."

"Enjoy it," I tell him, getting a good grip on his shoulders. He frowns, and I shove him hard. "In hell," I add as he falls backwards over the wall onto the street below.

I grab my bag and pull out a jumper and tracksuit bottoms. I slip them on and tuck my hair into a cap. I can hear screaming below as I gather everything up and make a run for the fire exit. I slam it closed and

# ARTHUR

rush down the stairs, all the way to the ground level. I push through some swing doors into a kitchen area. It's not been used for years, since the restaurant was bought out by the nightclub owners. I push out the exit and into a back alley which leads to the street beside the club. There are couples kissing and I dodge past them, breaking out into the busy street.

There's chaos as I calmly pass the nightclub entrance. The customers who are normally queuing outside to get in are all around the other side of the building, and as I pass, I see them crowded around Jeremy's lifeless body. Mobile phones are alight in the air as they hold them high above each other's heads to catch a glimpse. The youth of today have no compassion.

"What's happened?" I ask a girl who's sobbing into her hands.

"A man just jumped from the roof."

"Fuck. Is he okay?"

She wails, shaking her head. "No, he's dead."

# Chapter One

ARTHUR

"It's all over social media," says Tommy, the youngest of my brothers. He thrusts his mobile phone under my nose. "It went live on TikTok. Sick bastards," he adds.

It doesn't surprise me. Everything goes on social media these days, from someone's dinner to a messy breakup. Why should death escape the limelight? I pause the CCTV footage and sigh heavily. "Get her to me, now."

Tommy tucks his mobile phone away. "Albert already called her. She's on her way."

Albert, the second oldest and my right-hand man, is a godsend. Out of the four of us, we are the closest in age, and as brothers, it's always been that way. He's

# ARTHUR

always thinking two steps ahead of me, which makes my life easier.

Minutes later, the office door opens and in she walks. Rosey. Murderess, temptress, and batshit crazy employee. Although she'd argue we're business associates.

She plops herself down in the chair opposite me and lifts her feet onto the edge of my desk. Tommy raises an eyebrow in surprise, but I don't. She's got balls of steel and wouldn't think anything of her disrespectful move. "Whatcha."

"Whatcha?" I repeat, arching a brow. "Is that kid speak for hello?"

"Yeah, my kid keeps saying it. It's catchy."

I lean forward and sweep her feet from my desk. She sits up, straightening her back, ready for the fight that's about to ensue. "Fifteen minutes," I snap. "You took fifteen minutes to push him. What the fuck happened up there?"

"I like to talk, what can I say?"

I inhale loudly so she knows she is testing my patience. "You like to talk?" I repeat. "You like to fucking talk before you kill your target?" I yell the words, and she rolls her eyes. Why is she the only human I've come across who's not shit scared when I yell?

"We all do it differently. I'm sure you're a quick, clean-cut type of guy who wipes his blade and tucks it away neatly in his pocket. I like to talk."

I pinch the bridge of my nose. "Someone could have seen you and followed you up."

"They didn't."

"You take too many risks, Red."

She hates my nickname for her since she dyed her natural red hair to black. "I do it my way. I've been doing it my way for many years. If you don't like it, don't hire me." She rises to her feet.

"Sit the fuck down," I growl. She might be a part of The Perished Riders MC, but she's on my payroll and she'll leave when I tell her.

There's a knock on the door before she can respond and Albert comes in. "We're good. They have it down as suicide. Jumped to his death, apparently."

"Did you at least put the iPad back?" I ask, glaring at Rosey.

"Of course, I'm not an amateur."

"Remains to be seen. Next time I hire you to do a job, you do it quick and clean, then get the fuck out of there."

She gives a bored sigh, and Albert glances my way, probably wondering why I haven't killed her on the spot. "Have you transferred the money?" she asks.

"Yes. Now, leave. You're putting me in a bad mood."

# ARTHUR

"Do you think she's unhinged?" Tommy asks as we enter The Perished Riders clubhouse later. We often drop by to check in on business since we joined alliance with the club a couple of years ago.

"Who?"

"Rosey."

I groan. "Why are we still thinking about Red, brother? Don't be getting no ideas there. She's off the scale crazy."

"I wasn't," he says a little too quickly. "Just wondering is all. She's not scared of you, that's for sure."

I narrow my eyes, and he wilts. "She just hides it well, unlike you."

I shake hands with Maverick, the President of the club. "Busy in here tonight," I comment, looking around the packed-out bar of his clubhouse. I like Mav and his strong family values, it's what drew me to him. When he took over the club from his dad, he told me he was changing it, and he's done just that. There's still an undertone of criminal activity, but to the rest of London, he looks like he's cleaned the place up and he's putting good back into the community. I like that he doesn't flaunt his power. He doesn't need to—neither of us do. We have the

# NICOLA JANE

respect of the locals, and we're on good terms with all the important people who matter.

"Yeah, a brother got released. It's a big day."

"You want us to go?" I ask.

He shakes his head, laughing. "Man, you know you're more like one of the brothers. We call him Viking. You'll see why when he comes down from his room. His first priority was the club whores, of course. He's been away for ten years."

"Shit, assault?"

"Yeah. Wrongly." I laugh because all guys who end up inside plead innocence. Mav laughs too. "Long story," he adds.

Rosey passes us, winking at me. "See, not scared," whispers Tommy, nudging our shoulders together.

"I've seen that look in her eye before," Mav mutters. "Isn't she doing some work for you?" All club members, including the women, run extra work by him, so it makes sense he knows about our arrangement.

"She's a pain in my arse," I say, and Mav laughs. "No respect, no discipline. She just rocks up when she feels like it with a half-hearted plan. How the fuck she's gotten away with it for so long is beyond me."

"She's a wild child," says Mav, nodding. "She always was."

# ARTHUR

"You think my little brother can handle her?" I ask, slapping Tommy on the back.

Mav laughs harder. "Not a chance, but I'd pay to see it play out."

## MELI

"Tom Hardy would not be good in bed," Rosey argues. She's my closest friend, so I can forgive her for negative thoughts towards my future husband.

"Of course he would. Have you not seen his films?" I flick through Tom's pictures on my phone.

"Acting and actually doing are very different things. Anyway, why fantasise about a man you'll never meet? At least set your sights on someone you can touch. If it's violence and danger you want, look around, you're in an MC clubhouse."

I scan the room. I've known most of these men my entire life, and maybe that's the problem. My dad was once the club president, and now, that title has been passed down to my older brother. He's doing a much better job. "Around here, I'd be lucky to find anyone even half decent."

"At least these men are obtainable, so you can make it less of a fantasy and more a reality. It's been ages since you put yourself out there, Meli."

I scoff. "Sorry, 'Miss I go on a date every night'. Take your own advice."

"I'm out most nights," she argues.

## NICOLA JANE

"Killing and dating are not the same." Her career choice is not a nine-to-five office role. She always was a little crazy, so becoming a hitwoman wasn't a surprise to any of us.

She rolls her eyes. "I'm not interested in dating. Men are useless these days. I don't remember the last time I was swept off my feet. Actually, I do . . . it was never."

My mind wanders to Grim, the last man to sweep me off my feet, and that familiar ache returns to my chest. Not because I miss him, I honestly don't, but the pain I caused my sister was unforgivable, and although she's moved forward, and she and Grim are very happy together, I haven't forgiven myself so easily. It was a stupid little affair that got out of hand, and though we never did anything behind Hadley's back, we kept it a secret from her. She was so hurt after she found out, and she still doesn't quite look at me the same way, despite us being twins. I broke our bond over a man, and I hate myself for it.

"Earth to Meli," says Rosey, waving her hand in front of my face. "Are we going or not?"

"My god, have you girls seen this?" asks Gracie, holding her mobile phone in front of us. I take it from her and stare at the screen. It shows a crowd of people, and then it focusses on a body, lifeless on the ground.

# ARTHUR

"Christ, Gracie, what am I watching?" I ask, holding the phone farther away from my face.

"A guy jumped off Potters nightclub last night. It's all over social media," she replies.

I stare closer, wincing. "That's messed up."

Rosey doesn't seem interested, and my eyes widen. I wait for Gracie to move away before I turn on her. "That was you?" I accuse.

"Are we going out or not, because my heels already hurt and we haven't left."

"Why did you do that? I mean . . ." I can't find my words. "So, you just pushed him?"

"Meli, I can't discuss that crap with you. It's my job, move on."

"He probably had a wife and kids."

"No kids. Luckily."

"His wife must be devastated."

She sighs impatiently. "For someone who grew up in this MC, you're so fucking naïve." Her words sting, reminding me of my dad and his cruel comments. She realises the second she says them and covers her mouth. "Sorry. I didn't mean anything by that. Fuck. Can we just go and get drunk, please? We're good at that part."

I grab my bag. "Fine, but we're not going to Potters." She laughs at my response.

"Where are you going?" asks Mav, taking my arm and pulling me back to him.

"Out."

"Where?"

I groan. "I'm a grown-up, Mav. We can't keep having this conversation."

"Let her go," says Hadley as she passes us. "She's an adult, and she needs to find herself a man."

Mav releases me, giving me a knowing look. I don't think Hadley means it in a bad way, but she often drops comments like that, reminding me I'm not quite forgiven. Or maybe she just can't settle until I've shown I've moved on.

"Go to the club," says Arthur, handing me a pass. His fingers brush mine, and I get a familiar tingle in my stomach. Arthur flirts all the time. I used to think he was doing it to annoy Mav and Grim, but he's worse now than ever. If he knew my secrets, he wouldn't waste his time.

"Thanks," says Rosey, snatching the card from me and stuffing it in her bag.

Arthur shakes his head in annoyance and hands me a second pass. "Maybe I'll see you there later." His words are laced with promise, and I give a weak smile. Men like Arthur Taylor don't date women like me. They *use* women like me, and I don't want to be the reason Mav and him fall out.

As we step outside, Rosey grins. "He flirts with you."

# ARTHUR

"He flirts with loads of women. Have you seen him at the club? He's got 'bad guy' written all over him. Besides, Mav would kill him."

"Well, if you're not going there, I might." She winks and walks ahead, waving her hand at a passing cab.

I crumple the card in my hand. Rosey fits with Arthur, and she'd be perfect with him, so I don't know why that thought bothers me.

ARTHUR

Despite what people think, I'm not good at talking to women. Albert says it's because I'm too direct and bossy. I don't ask, I order. But that's just the way I am. You don't get to run all the areas in London that I do without having authority. It's also the reason I'm single.

I walk through the main entrance to one of my six nightclubs. This one, Artie's, is my favourite. I do most of my work from the office here. I fist bump the doormen as I pass. They're my most loyal security and have been with me from the beginning, when all I ran was the door security on other people's premises.

I make my way past reception, leaving Tommy speaking to Joanna to check ticket sales. It's Saturday night, so I expect the place to be heaving, and I'm right. The lower bar area is crammed full of students and other young people, all trying to get their one-pound shots lined up before eleven, when the offer ends and the drinks go back up to full price. It works well to get them in the club, and by eleven, they can't be bothered to leave and find anywhere else, so they party here until closing at three a.m.

Taking the stairs two at a time, I brush shoulders with several drunk customers heading back down to the ground floor. The second floor is just as busy. The music's different on each level and the dance music blaring up here is popular.

I bypass the chaos and take the next set of stairs to the VIP area. I kiss the hostess on the cheek. "Business good?" I ask, and she nods, turning the sign-in book towards me.

"Almost to capacity in there," she replies.

"Glad to hear it," I say as my eyes scan the list. Amelia and Rosey both signed in an hour ago. "Were these two alone?" I ask, tapping next to their names. Angie nods. "Great, thanks."

I push open the large black doors. I had them shipped in from Italy, like most of the furniture in here. I wanted mysterious and dark, with different shades of black and red, and everyone knows most of the best-made furniture comes from Italy.

I shake hands with a few of our members as I pass by. The VIP annual fee is eye-watering, but it keeps out the riffraff. Besides, they get treated like

## ARTHUR

kings and queens here, from champagne on arrival to canapés prepared by one of London's top chefs. I have police officers, judges, and even members of parliament signed up. Most of them bring their younger knock-offs as it makes them look cool having a membership to somewhere exclusive. Others come here to find their next sidepiece. If they knew their hard-earned wages went right back into running my guns and drugs over the city, maybe they wouldn't pay . . . or maybe they would. After all, crime keeps them in a job.

I get to my usual spot beside the bar. I like this corner because it's dark, shading me from everyone else. Sometimes when I come here, I need to just watch without being fist bumped or back slapped. It's like I'm anonymous, and it's surprising what you see when no one knows you're watching.

A drink is placed down without me asking. I nod my head in thanks and raise the glass to my lips. I hear Meli before I see her. She's laughing at something Red is saying in her ear. Red is the female version of myself but with a lot less control. She speaks what she thinks and doesn't apologise for it, and I like that about her. But Meli, there's something about her that makes me stop and stare whenever she's around. She's loud and outspoken, though maybe not as much as her friend, but I see through it because it's a front. She plays the part of someone oozing confidence, and when she walks into a room, she makes sure all eyes are on her. Yet the times when she's sitting back, unnoticed and unseen, her mind wanders off somewhere else, somewhere dark. Her eyes stare blankly and, occasionally, she flinches. There's pain there. A lot of pain.

I've probed Maverick about it before, but he doesn't open up about his sisters. I don't blame him. I wouldn't want to tell me either. I'm no good for her, and we both know it.

"Penny for them," says our newest barmaid, Alicia. She's leaning over to me, and her tits are spilling out of the skimpy black uniform. She's definitely gone a size too small, and I make a mental note to speak to my bar manager about it. The image in my VIP area is important.

"It's busy," I tell her, a hint to get her back to the waiting customers instead of trying to pick me up.

She glances over her shoulder and then back to me. "Yeah."

"So, you should get back to it," I push.

She's already drawn attention to my quiet spot, and as Marcus, one of my long-term employees, comes over to order her back to work, Rosey appears. "Do you always hide in dark corners?" she asks, smirking.

"Your speciality, I believe."

# ARTHUR

"It's all very well having VIP tickets, but why am I still having to queue at the bar?"

"You'd think with all the money you just acquired, you'd be able to pay the yearly membership," I say, clicking my fingers to get Marcus's attention. "Priority ladies," I tell him. "Serve them first."

"Not a problem," he replies. "What can I get you both?"

"Is it on your tab?" Meli asks, cocking a brow and giving me a cheeky grin.

I roll my eyes. "Set them up a tab, I'll settle it," I tell Marcus. He laughs, entering the details into the computer as Meli fires her order.

"Were you a little impressed?" asks Rosey, leaning closer to me. She smells amazing.

"With?" I ask, even though I know what she's asking. Was I impressed with the way she shoved Jeremy Hall off the top of a building, making the world think he jumped?

"The first job you hired me for."

I think on her words, and she watches me closely. "It was clean. No ties. You have the assets to lure a man to his death without him realising, which makes it an easy kill. So, I don't know if impressed is the right word. Pleased, maybe."

She looks annoyed. Maybe she's used to men praising her. "By assets, you mean tits and arse?" I nod, sipping my drink. "I can kill a man without those."

"So, you lured Jeremy Hall to his death by force? You dragged him up those stairs, onto a roof, and heaved him over the edge?"

"Well, not in this instance, no. But I can when I want to."

"Don't be offended, Red. I didn't hire you for your brute strength. I have people for that. You did a good job. I wouldn't have paid you otherwise."

# Chapter Two

MELI

Maybe I should have told her that actually I do quite like Arthur. He's all wrong for me. Of course, he is because I always go for the wrong ones. But he's good looking and strong, and not in a muscle-head, gym addict kind of way, but he's got that look about him that tells you he can end you in a second and not even break out in a sweat. He's powerful, and he'd probably protect me from . . . well, I don't really know what I need protecting from because I'm surrounded by bikers day and night. But despite that, I never feel truly safe.

I watch how Rosey leans into Arthur so she can hear his deep, gravelly voice. It's the type of voice that makes you shiver right down to your toes. I wonder what they're talking about. They're both a little crazy—Rosey in a Harley Quinn kind of way, and Arthur in a deadly silent yet scary kind of way. It's why, in my eyes, they're perfectly matched.

Rosey is pulling her moves. The ones she lays on any man she fancies, laughing and flicking her hair. Arthur gives nothing away, not even a smile to show he's interested. She turns to me. "I need to pee. Be right back."

I stand awkwardly, feeling Arthur's eyes on me. "You're quiet," he states.

"That's me, little quiet one."

He laughs, and my heart stutters in my chest. It's not often he does it, but he really should. I want to hear him laugh all the time. "How's things?"

He never asks me that stuff. He flirts, sort of. He isn't good at it, but that's just Arthur. I don't suppose he needs to flirt because women must throw themselves at him all the time. I frown and answer, "Good, I guess."

"Good, you guess?" he repeats. "Tell me, why haven't you settled down like your sister?" My heart does that twisty thing again. I hate talking about it because I know Arthur knows what happened. Everyone knows.

"I'm not the settling down type."

"You don't want a husband and kids?"

"Nope. I love partying too much."

# ARTHUR

He tips his head to one side. "Funny, because you don't look like you're having a good time right now."

I scoff. "Because I'm the third wheel."

"Does that bother you, Amelia?" The way he says my name makes me breathless. It rolls off his tongue and somehow sounds sexy. I have a sudden urge to hear it whispered close to my ear, to feel his hot breath on my skin.

"What did I miss?" asks Rosey, stepping between us and breaking the spell.

I smile and down my drink. "Absolutely nothing. I was just telling Arthur I'm going to find myself a hot, sexy, rich man, so you guys enjoy yourselves." I turn and walk off into the crowd.

---

I'm too hot. I've spent the last hour dancing and my feet are beginning to throb. I lean down and snatch my heel off my left foot, then my right, and make my way through the sweaty bodies to find the bathroom.

I take the first door I see and head up the stairs, opening the door at the end and scowling when I'm on the roof space and not in the bathroom. "Fuck," I mutter. I'm desperate to pee, and the cold air only worsens the urge to go. I glance around and find there's no one up here, so I take my chances and

# NICOLA JANE

scoot off to the far corner. Dropping my bag and shoes nearby, I hitch up my skirt and pull down my knickers. Then, I crouch in an unladylike manner and sigh in relief. I shouldn't have drunk so much.

"Yah know, there's a great bathroom in this establishment. It has toilets and everything."

I jump in fright, unable to stop now I'm mid-flow and feeling completely embarrassed that I've been caught by the owner. Arthur doesn't turn away. Instead, he watches as I finish up and pull my knickers back into place.

"I was trying to find the bathroom," I explain. "I'm so sorry."

He grins. "If you've gotta go, you've gotta go. I'll have my bar manager check the signs are lit up." He leans over the wall, resting his arms on it and peering down at the ground below. "Do you ever get intrusive thoughts, Meli?" he asks.

I take it as a sign he doesn't want me to leave right away, so I join him, looking down at the crowded London street below. "Everyone does."

"You think?" he asks, tipping his head to the side and looking at me. I nod. "I often sit up here and wonder what it would feel like to throw myself over the edge."

I half smile. "It's a long way down."

"Do you think people change their mind halfway down?"

# ARTHUR

I nod again. "Probably. The realisation must hit them, but then it's too late. They can't claw their way back. I think you have to be brave to kill yourself." His eyes find me again, waiting for me to continue. "Most people think it's the coward's way out, but I think you have to process a lot to come to that decision. I mean, most people plan it, right? They buy the pills or the rope and choose when to do it and where. They sometimes write a note to say goodbye. That takes balls. You know you're going to end your life and you're never coming back. It's a huge decision. Probably one of the biggest." I pull myself up onto the wall. It's thick enough to sit on comfortably, but Arthur watches me with caution.

"Fuck, Meli, don't throw yourself over the edge. Mav would kill me."

I grin. "He'd want to know what you were doing up on the roof with his sister for a start."

He laughs, taking a step back and moving to stand in front of me. He gently picks up my bare foot and begins to rub it. I close my eyes as he works the ache away with his skilful fingers. "I'd tell him you were peeing on my roof."

"And your reason as to why I ended up over the edge?" I ask.

"I'd say you'd had enough of the monsters in your head and felt too sad to carry on."

## NICOLA JANE

His words pull at my heart, and my eyes meet his. He knows. He knows I'm sad. "What monsters?" I whisper.

He takes my other foot and gives it the same treatment. It crosses my mind he could tip me over the edge without a second thought, yet I'm not even a little nervous, and I realise I trust him. "The ones that visit you at night. That steal your good dreams and remind you of all the bad times. The times he didn't protect you when he should have." My eyes fill with tears and I frown, unsure where they've come from. He doesn't know the truth, only close family do, so how the hell did he get it so accurate?

"What would be your reason to jump?" I ask, changing the subject and blinking to clear my eyes.

He ponders my question. "To find peace."

"Peace from what?"

He smiles sadly. "We all have monsters, Meli."

I inhale sharply, hating the way our talk has turned so dark. I pull my foot from his hand, jump down off the wall, and stand in front of him. "You know what you need?" I ask, swooping down to pick up my bag and shoes. "A good woman to distract you. Where did Rosey go?" I brush past him and head for the exit, not waiting to see if he follows.

## ARTHUR

# ARTHUR

Meli's definitely giving me mixed signals. One second, she's watching me from across the room, and I swear it's longingly. And the next, she's pushing me towards Rosey. And Rosey is making it very apparent I'm on her radar. I can't decide if that's a turn-on or not.

I step back into the VIP area, and Rosey holds up a drink for me. I head over, occasionally being stopped on the way. "You don't look like the type to dance?" She says it more like a question.

I smirk. "No, I don't dance."

She sips her drink. "No, I imagine you have people for that. Rumour has it you have a secret room back there." She nods her head in the direction of doors that do indeed lead to private rooms.

"For dancing?"

She laughs. "You tell me. I imagine you have women back there tied to your bed." She runs my tie through her fingers, and I picture the way she was with her last victim. I watched the CCTV images of when she seduced Jeremy Hall, right before I deleted them. I can't ignore my reaction to her—she definitely has some kind of bewitching skill.

"Is that a fantasy, Red?" She doesn't blush. She never does. Not like Meli.

"Maybe." She smirks before downing the rest of her drink.

## NICOLA JANE

I indicate for Marcus to get her another, which he does. "The private rooms are for various things," I tell her. "Meetings, impressing important people—"

"Important people you have sex with?" I smirk. She's too forward, and I never have to guess what's on her mind because she tells me. "I'd like to see the rooms."

Meli joins us, her cheeks flushed from too much alcohol and dancing. "My feet are killing me," she tells Rosey. "Can we go?"

Rosey narrows her eyes, trying to communicate a message to her friend that I suspect involves me. "I just got a new drink."

Meli rolls her eyes, and when she remains standing by us, Rosey looks more irritated. I grab Meli by the waist, pulling her to me, and she lets out a surprised squeal. I lift her onto the bar and again take her foot in my hands and begin rubbing. Rosey watches the interaction with curiosity.

"Arthur was just telling me about his private rooms over there," Rosey says, nodding in the general direction.

"You have private rooms?" asks Meli.

"They're occupied right now," I say, swapping to Meli's other foot. She rests her hands behind her and lets her head fall back in pleasure. I don't think she realises how sexy she looks. She has the attention of

# ARTHUR

men queuing at the bar, and I've never wanted to blind a group of people as much as I do right now.

"Maybe our next meeting could be in one," Rosey suggests.

Meli frowns. "You two have meetings?"

I glare at Rosey, waiting to see how she'll get out of this because no one should know the agreement we have. "No, Meli, I was trying to flirt, but thanks for ruining it." She drains her glass and slams it on the bar. "Let's go." She grabs Meli's shoes and practically shoves them into her stomach. Meli catches them, looking confused. I lift her from the bar and slowly slide her down my body, feeling every soft curve against my hard torso. Her eyes flutter up to meet mine, and I know she feels the spark flying back and forth between us by her sharp intake of breath.

"I'll walk you both out and get my driver to drop you home."

---

I slam my laptop closed and glance at the bright LED on the wall clock. Six a.m. The club's been closed for two hours and I'm still here looking over the books. I stare at the spare desk across from me and sigh at the amount of paperwork stacked up there. I really need to hire someone to deal with that.

# NICOLA JANE

I stand and close the blinds. The sun is just rising, and I need to get some shut-eye before my day begins again. Dropping down on the couch, I close my eyes, and the first person I see is Meli. I smile to myself. Fuck, I'd probably sleep a hell of a lot more if I had someone like her waiting in my bed.

---

I'm woken when the office door slams open. I sit up, alarmed for a second until I get my bearings. My brother, Albert, stares at me. "Why are you sleeping in here?"

I squint as he opens the blinds and daylight streams in. "What time is it?"

"Eleven."

"Shit. I have a meeting." I get up and go to the built-in closet. After finding a fresh shirt and trousers, I head for the bathroom attached to my office and shower in record time. When I return to the office, Albert is entertaining Jolene Hall. She's dressed in black, playing the part of a grieving wife well. She rises to her feet gracefully, and we shake hands. "Nice place you have here," she remarks. We usually meet in bars that aren't owned by me.

"Thanks." I take a seat behind my desk, and she sits back down. "Any updates?"

# ARTHUR

"Yes. It's not being investigated. The police believe he jumped. They found the videos and photographs on his iPad, and they think he couldn't live with his dirty fucking secret." She spits the words with anger.

"Best outcome for all." I stand, indicating the meeting is over, but she hesitates.

"Actually, I might need your help again."

"For?"

"A similar thing. I want rid of someone."

"You know I need more details than that."

She glances at Albert, showing she's uncomfortable. I nod at him to leave, which he does. "I've been seeing this man."

"No. I can't possibly wipe somebody else out with a connection to you. How would it look?"

"No one knows about us. It wouldn't lead back to me."

"No. My answer is no."

"I'll double the money."

I sigh heavily. "What exactly has he done?"

"Used me."

I laugh. "If I wiped out every motherfucker who used a woman, the male population would deplete, including myself."

"He used me to get information on my brothers. And now he has, he's blackmailing me."

I groan. "Have you ever thought of staying celibate? You have terrible taste in men."

"My brothers can't find out about this. And if this guy follows through on his threats, we'll all be in the shit."

"Jesus, Jolene, what the fuck does he have on you?"

"I told him about Jeremy. I didn't mean to. I was just telling him we had the all-clear to go public, so he asked questions and it came out. He recorded me."

I pinch the bridge of my nose. "I can't keep that from your brothers." I pull out my phone, and she dives at me, trying to grab it. "Fuck's sake," I growl, taking her wrists and pinning her to the desk. Albert hears the commotion and comes back. "Hold this bitch while I make a call," I snap.

Max, her eldest brother, answers straight away. "Arthur, is it wise you call me on my personal phone?"

"I have your sister here," I say, ignoring his remark. "I think you should get over to Artie's right now."

"On the way," he mutters, knowing it's urgent by the tone of my voice.

By the time he arrives, along with their brother, Leon, I have Jolene calmer with her hands tied behind her back. Max arches a brow when he sees her. "There better be a fucking good reason you have my sister tied up."

"Be happy I haven't killed her," I snap.

# ARTHUR

"What's she done now?" asks Leon, cutting the tape from her wrists. She remains seated.

"She told her lover about Jeremy." They both glare at her, and she shrinks back in her chair. "And now, he's blackmailing her."

"I don't know what's wrong with you," snaps Leon, slapping her across the face. I wince. I hate violence against women, but it's their business. "What exactly does he want?"

"Money," she sobs. "Fifty grand."

"You fucking idiot," hisses Max as he slams a piece of paper on my desk. "Write his name." She does it. "Can we do anything about this?" He directs the question at me.

I take the piece of paper and laugh. "You gotta be shitting me." I show Max and Leon.

"You're fucking one of the E15 boys?" Max yells. It's bad news. If we take this guy out, we'll go to a street war with his associated gang, and those kinds of wars aren't worth our time. Their members are fearless, feral, and cocky. They use younger kids to do their dirty work so they never get caught, and the war will be chaotic and messy, something myself or Max could do without.

"I'll see what I can do, but I can't take him out. My days of street wars are over," I say. "What did he record you on?"

"His mobile phone. He has two, a burner and his smartphone. It's on that."

"Would he likely make a copy?"

She shakes her head. "No, he isn't that clever."

"He was clever enough to record you," snaps Leon.

"Let's hope a threat works," I mutter. "Cos if I get pulled up in this, I'm coming for you all," I warn, glaring at Max. He nods once, grabbing his sister by her upper arm and dragging her to the door. "And Max," he looks back to me, "sort her out. This can't happen again. I expect double payment wired direct to me within an hour."

Albert slams the door closed after they leave. "Fuck, we don't need this, Art."

"Tell me about it, but I'm not worried. This kid's not even an elder. He's a chancer after some cash, and I doubt his bosses even know. I'll come with you to visit him personally. A quick warning should be enough for him to realise his luck's done."

# Chapter Three

MELI

I finish tying the last pink bow in my three-year-old niece's hair and smile at her reflection in the mirror. "You look gorgeous," I tell her, kissing her on the head.

Grim passes us and his eyes fall to his daughter. "Is she wearing lip gloss?"

"Don't I look pretty, Daddy?" asks Oakley, pouting. I wince, knowing I'm going to get the blame for that little pose. Grim sits down on a nearby chair and narrows his eyes, ready to give me the full lecture, but then Hadley enters the room and I immediately stand and begin to pack away the hairbrushes and makeup. It's been years since she discovered I'd slept with Grim, but I still feel uncomfortable being seen together. So now, whenever Grim is near me, I feel this overwhelming urge to put distance between us because I'd hate for her to think I'd ever do anything like that again.

Grim realises she's there too and rolls his eyes. "Jesus, Meli, you keep jumping up like that and she'll think we have something to hide."

"I don't want her to see us talking. It might upset her," I hiss.

"It was years ago. I think she's over it," he mutters, his voice full of sarcasm.

"Women don't just get over that sort of thing, Grim."

Hadley wanders over and smiles lovingly at Oakley, who performs a little twirl and pout just for her. "Wow, look at you."

"Yes, look at her," snaps Grim, "with lip gloss on."

"Well, I think you look very pretty," says Hadley, picking her daughter up and nuzzling into her neck.

"You don't think she's a little young for makeup?" Grim asks, arching a brow.

"Hardly makeup, Grim," says Hadley with a laugh. "Besides, Aunt Meli is good at makeovers, isn't she, sweetie?"

Oakley nods, and I find myself smiling. "Glad you're happy, madam," I say, kissing her on the cheek. "Can I get back to what I was doing before you rudely demanded my attention?" I tease.

# ARTHUR

"Meli has a boyfriend," Oakley announces, and Hadley grins as she eyes me suspiciously.

"Does she now?"

"No, she doesn't," I say. "And if she did, why would she tell her blabbermouth niece about it?"

"Does Mav know?" asks Grim.

"There is no boyfriend."

"Who was the man on your phone?" asks Oakley innocently, and Hadley grins wider. Oakley caught me checking out pictures of Arthur on one of his business websites. I feel my cheeks flush with embarrassment, which only makes Hadley laugh harder.

"Oakley, I'll tell Daddy your secret if you don't stay quiet."

Now, it's Oakley's turn to blush because there's no way she'd want Grim finding out she has a boyfriend at nursery, even if he is only four years old. Grim takes his daughter from Hadley's arms and sweeps her away, promising to tickle her until she confesses all.

"So," says Hadley, falling into the seat Grim vacated, "who is he?"

"No one. I was looking at pictures on the web, and she must have thought it was a boyfriend. Kids." I roll my eyes.

"You forget I know that look, Amelia," she says. "There's someone."

Rosey skips over. "Does this jacket go with the outfit?" she asks.

"Yeah, you look lovely," Hadley replies.

"You look nice. Off anywhere special?" I ask, hoping to change the subject.

"Maybe," she says, grinning.

The door opens and Arthur Taylor walks in looking smouldering hot in shades and a suit, his expensive Rolex gleaming on his wrist. "Oh my god, are you going on a date with Arthur?" whispers Hadley excitedly.

Again, Rosey grins. "Maybe," she repeats.

"A date?" I ask, feeling my heart sink to my stomach.

"And here I was thinking the man has no heart," Hadley comments. "Since when were you into him?"

"You're not blind, Hads. The man's gorgeous, and if he's asking me out for a date, I'm not gonna turn him down," Rosey says with a wink.

She saunters off in his direction. "Don't do anything we wouldn't," Hadley shouts after her.

I watch the way Arthur places a protective hand on Rosey's lower back, guiding her out the door. "Oh wow, it's him?" Hadley gasps.

I bring my attention back to her. "Huh?"

"Arthur . . . you like him."

## ARTHUR

I don't immediately answer because I'm still trying to work out why my heart feels so heavy. "Don't be stupid. Rosey's into him."

"That doesn't mean you're not."

"It means he's off-limits." We both fall silent, knowing the last man I went after was also off-limits. "I learned my lesson," I add quietly.

"Meli," she whispers, sounding sad, "that's in the past. We've all moved on. Does Rosey know how you feel?"

I scoff, bending to pick up my things. "No, because I don't feel anything for Arthur Taylor. He's a criminal and bossy, he charms women into his bed, and—" I stop talking as a man's shoes come into view. I trail my eyes up the grey suit trousers, over the crisp white shirt, and clocking the gold Rolex until my eyes reach Arthur's.

"Don't let me stop you," he says, folding his arms over his chest and staring, waiting for me to continue.

I swallow the lump in my throat. "Did you forget something?" I ask, my voice coming out high-pitched and squeaky.

"I thought I had, but I changed my mind," he says coldly before turning and heading back out.

Hadley stares up at me with large, unblinking eyes. "Fuck. What do you think he came back to say?" I shrug, acting like I don't care he just caught

# NICOLA JANE

me slagging him off. "What if he was gonna ask you on a date?"

I screw my face up in disgust. "With Rosey waiting outside for him? That's low. He doesn't think of me like that. Rosey is much more his type."

"Because they're both psychos?" she asks.

We giggle. "Exactly."

## ARTHUR

I pull out a chair for Rosey to sit before taking the one opposite her. I like to have business meetings over dinner. If Rosey ever gets caught in her line of work, I can pass this off as a date, while a meeting at my office looks more suspicious.

The waiter pours us each a glass of wine and takes our order. I wait for him to leave before starting. "I have another proposition," I tell her.

"Can't we at least eat before we talk business?"

"It's a business meeting, so it's all business," I remind her. "It's not a full job. He gets to walk away." She sighs. "I need you to lure him to me."

"Not really my thing, Arthur. I like clean jobs where they don't get to talk after."

"I forgot, you like to do all the talking before they die," I say sarcastically. "He's got something I need. I want you to get that from him, and then I'll come in and finish the job off. He's just a kid trying to be a big man, nothing to worry about, and it's good money."

# ARTHUR

"That's not clean. By then, he'll have seen my face and yours. What does he have?"

"A recording on his smartphone."

"Can't I just break in and take the phone?"

"If it were that simple, I'd do it myself. But this guy needs to know he's got to keep his mouth shut. If he begins shouting his mouth off . . . well, it won't be good."

"So, you want me to take his phone, lure him to you, and you'll threaten him?" I nod. "What exactly is on the phone?"

"You know that's not how I work, Red. I give you the details you need to know. What's on that phone is irrelevant."

She shrugs out of her jacket and my eyes are drawn to her breasts. It's the effect she was after because she smirks. "Focus, Arthur." I swallow and loosen my tie. "Aren't you too high up the chain for this kind of thing?" she asks. "Beating people up seems so amateur."

I nod in agreement. "Trust me, it wasn't on my list of things to do this week, but it came up. Seeing me should be enough to let him know he's pushed his luck too far."

## NICOLA JANE

After lunch, I take Rosey back to the clubhouse, making my way through to see Maverick. I halt mid-step when Meli comes running from the kitchen, slamming right into my chest. I steady her, and her giggles fade as her eyes reach mine. Ollie, Rosey's son, is behind her, and before he can stop, he throws something white in the air. It hits Meli on the back and sprays up, covering us both in flour. "Oh shit," she whispers, trying hard not to laugh. "I am so sorry."

"Sorry, Mr. Taylor," Ollie splutters. "I didn't mean to get you."

"Yet you did," I mutter dryly, releasing Meli and shaking my arm.

"Don't brush it," Meli says, gripping my jacket and pulling it from my shoulders. "You'll make it worse."

She hands the Armani jacket to Ollie. "Here, take this to Mama B and tell her it's Arthur's. She'll get it good as new." She then turns to me. "You can wash your hair in my bathroom."

I follow her up the stairs. "If I didn't know better, I'd think you were enjoying this," I say, noting she's still trying hard not to laugh.

"It was an accident, but your face was a picture," she says, giggling again. The sound rings in my ears and warms my heart.

I stop in the doorway to her bedroom. I've never been past the ground floor in the club, and I've

# ARTHUR

certainly never been inside Meli's bedroom. I take in the pink . . . so much pink. There's twinkling lights and fake blossoms on one wall. She looks back to see why I've stopped, then she looks embarrassed. "Excuse the room. It's the teenage room I never had. I love blossoms, I love spring, and this is the result of that."

I nod slowly, entering and closing the door. "It's very . . . Meli."

"Bathroom is through there," she says, pointing.

I go in that direction and close the door. I take off my shirt and hang in on a hook next to something black and lacey. Feeling the garment in my fingers, I resist the urge to press it to my nose. I lean my head under the shower and turn it on, rinsing my hair which makes a flour paste. I feel around for shampoo, squirting it onto my head. The apple scent that's all Meli fills the air and a warm sensation builds in my chest. Overhearing her words to her sister earlier pissed me off. She grew up in an MC for fuck's sake, yet she's judging me on my line of work. But now, being in her private space and smelling her, I can almost forget what she said.

I turn off the shower and grab a towel, rubbing my hair as I go back into her bedroom and find her sitting on her bed. She stares at me, letting her eyes run over my chest, and I see the hunger in them. I move around the room like I'm unaffected by her watching me with heat.

I stop by a group of photographs pinned to her wall. There are some of her and Hadley as kids, a few of her and Mama B, and some of Oakley. "No man on your wall of fame?" I ask, knowing Mav makes dating hard for her.

She laughs, but it's empty of humour. "How was your date with Rosey?"

"Date?" I repeat, running my fingers over her dresser to a pile of makeup. "You have a lot of make-up." Doesn't she realise she doesn't need a drop of it?

"Didn't you two just go on a date?"

"Is that what Rosey said?" I open the first drawer to find more makeup. I can't tell Meli it was business, but I also don't want her to think it was a date.

"Just look after her, okay. She's vulnerable, despite how she acts."

"What does all this stuff do?" I ask, holding up a bottle of something liquid and beige.

She comes up behind me and takes the bottle from my hand. "That's foundation, to hide all the bags under my eyes." She places it back in the drawer.

"You don't have dark circles, Meli." I pick up something else, and she sighs.

"Mascara."

# ARTHUR

"And you need ten tubes of that?" I drop it back and close the drawer.

"Makeup for every occasion."

I open the second drawer, and she tries to slam it closed, but I've already spotted what she doesn't want me to see. Her hand falls away and she groans. I smirk, pulling out the large purple vibrator. I hold it up between us, arching a brow. "Amongst your makeup?"

She covers her face with her hands. "Aren't you supposed to be meeting with Mav or something?" she asks through her fingers.

I put her toy back in its place and close the drawer. Then I take her wrists, pulling her hands away from her face. Sparks ignite where our skin touches, and I have to shake my head to clear it. "Don't be embarrassed about taking care of business, Angel. And for the record, you don't need the makeup. You're gorgeous with or without it." I release her before I do something I shouldn't and go back into the bathroom, grabbing my shirt and slipping it on. As I head for the door, she watches me. "Also, it wasn't a date with Rosey." I leave with those words hanging between us.

I step into the hall, fastening my shirt, and when I look up, Rosey is watching me with her mouth open. She glances at Meli's bedroom door, then back to me again. "Careful, Red, you might catch a fly." I go

47

down the stairs without explaining myself because I don't feel the need to. She shouldn't have told Meli we went on a date.

# Chapter Four

MELI

I'm still clutching my hands over my racing heart when the door opens and Rosey comes in. She eyes me suspiciously. "You don't look just fucked," she comments.

"S'cuse me?"

"I just bumped into Arthur in the hall. He was fastening his shirt." She arches her brow, waiting for my response.

"Oh, that." I force a laugh. "Ollie flour bombed him. It was so embarrassing. He washed his hair in my bathroom."

"Thank god for that, I honestly thought you'd stolen him from me." She laughs, flopping down on my bed.

# NICOLA JANE

Her words annoy me, especially seeing as Arthur didn't see their lunch as a date. "Is he technically yours for me to steal?"

"I called first dibs," she says, checking her mobile phone.

"First dibs?" I repeat, scoffing. "We're not in school, Rosey."

She looks up from her mobile. "Do you like him or something?"

"No, of course not. I'm just saying that maybe you need to stop seeing him as yours when he's not."

"I'm manifesting him," she replies, grinning. "He'll be mine."

"How did the date go?" I ask.

She rolls onto her back, staring up at the ceiling. "Do you think he's into me?"

I note she's ignoring my question. "I don't know, Rosey. Has anything happened between you?" I hold my breath, waiting for her answer.

"No. I mean, we flirt. A lot. Maybe he's shy. I should just go for it, right?"

"Depends on what you mean by that. Some guys hate forward women. I don't get why you're suddenly so into him."

She shrugs. "He gets the whole career thing. Most men are put off by that."

"Career?" I repeat, smirking.

# ARTHUR

She scowls. "Just because it's not on the career advisor's list doesn't mean it's not a career. I mean, they should totally add it. We could rid the world of evil."

"We have people for that, Rosey—they're called the police force and the judicial system."

She laughs. "Not everything can be solved in the right way." She pauses. "Speaking of work, I need you to come to a party with me later. Long story, but I can't turn up on my own and I have to be there."

I shrug. It's not like I have anything better to do. "Okay. Casual or smart?"

"Completely casual. I'm talking jeans and trainers."

---

I stare wide-eyed out of the cab window. We had to sneak out of the clubhouse tonight because, for whatever reason, Rosey didn't want to tell Mav where the party was. And as the cab rolls to a stop, I realise why. "We can't get out here," I hiss.

"Relax, no one knows us."

"So, why are we here?"

Rosey pays the driver, and we get out. She links arms with me. "I have a really quick job to do."

I pull away from her. "What?" I screech. She shushes me, glancing around to make sure we haven't got anyone's attention. She's right to be worried because this part of town isn't a place we should hang out. It's known for its out-of-control crime rate and gang problems. It's not run by anyone like Mav or Arthur. It's left to the street gangs to fight it out. "You took a job here?"

"It's not my usual job. Everyone walks away alive."

"You hope, cos if these guys find out who we are, *who I am*, we definitely won't walk out of here alive."

"Arthur knows about it," she reassures me. "It's all under control." I relax a little. If Arthur knows, we'll be safe.

We head towards a block of high-rise flats. Music blares out from several of them, and shouting can be heard amongst crying children. Teenagers whizz past on bikes and scooters, probably ferrying drugs across the estate.

We take the stairs, and I cover my nose. It smells of urine, and we occasionally have to step around a homeless person sleeping in the stairwell.

We reach the third floor and move along the passage. The music is louder, and people are hanging around outside one of the flats. "If anyone asks, Jordan invited us."

"Is that a male or female?"

She shrugs. "I have no idea, Meli. I'm just assuming there's a Jordan here."

# ARTHUR

"You mean there's no Jordan at all? We haven't been invited?" I hiss.

"Take a goddamn breath and chill the fuck out. Stick with me and it's going to be fine."

We get stopped at the door by a large man with his face half-covered behind a scarf. "Who are you?" he grunts.

"JC and Amy," says Rosey. "Jordan told us to come."

"Which Jordan? The male or female one?"

I snigger, earning a jab in the ribs from her elbow. "The male," she says. He nods and moves to the side so we can go in. The flat is crammed with hot, sweaty bodies. The music is too loud, and I wonder if it bothers the other tenants or if they all do this sort of thing.

We go to the kitchen, where the sink is full of beers, and Rosey grabs us each one. We lean against the worktop, and she scans the place. "Okay, the guy I need to get to is with someone," she tells me, and I follow her line of sight to a man chatting to a woman.

"I need to get him by himself. Can you distract her?"

"No," I say firmly, shaking my head. "She looks feral, like she could definitely kick my arse."

Rosey sighs, thinking of a plan. "Okay, just follow me," she mutters, heading their way. When we're right behind the girl, Rosey tips her beer down the

# NICOLA JANE

girl's back, and the second she turns around, Rosey glares at me. "Fuck's sake, Amy, watch it." I stare wide-eyed back at her, and she smirks and turns to the girl who is screaming. "I am so sorry. She's drunk. It was an accident. Amy, go and help her sort her top out," Rosey adds, staring at me.

I'm shaking with a mixture of anger and terror as I follow the girl to a bathroom. We get inside, and she immediately takes the top off. "Sorry," I mutter feebly.

"It's fine," she tells me, and I relax a little. "You did me a favour cos Dylan was chatting me up and he makes my skin crawl." She shudders for added effect.

"Take mine," I tell her, shrugging out of my jacket and removing my top.

"You sure?" she asks, eyeing the lace bodice underneath.

"I have a jacket, and this is something I'd wear on a night out, so I don't mind." I put my jacket back on.

When we re-join Rosey, she's kissing the guy. "You should warn your friend. He's a dick," the girl tells me.

Rosey pulls back and puts her arm around my shoulder. "Here's my friend, Amy. Let's all go back to hers." He nods eagerly. I have no idea what her plan is, but I find myself following the pair out of the party flat and up two floors to another flat. The

# ARTHUR

door isn't locked, and we walk right in. I note we can still hear the music from downstairs.

"This your place?" he asks me, frowning, and I nod. "Cos I ain't seen you round here before."

"She just moved in," Rosey says, grabbing his face and pulling him in for another kiss. It does the trick because he's distracted enough to stop questioning me. "Where's your phone? I'll put my number in it."

I move through to the kitchen, leaving Rosey to do whatever she's been hired to do. I try to turn on the light, but it doesn't come on, and then suddenly, a hand covers my mouth and I'm pulled against a hard body. "It's me," whispers Arthur. I stop struggling, but he doesn't release me. Instead, he pushes me against the wall, pressing his body to mine. "Why are you here?" He sounds annoyed, but he uncovers my mouth so I can answer.

"Rosey asked me to come."

His hand moves to my waist, and when he feels the lace material, he rips my jacket open and stares down at the bodice. "Where are your clothes?" he snaps.

"Long story."

"Hate to break it up, but it's showtime," whispers another voice from across the room. Albert steps into the moonlight.

"Stay here, Angel. Do not come into that room," Arthur orders, and I nod. He stares at me for a moment longer, and I swear he looks like he's about to kiss me, but a commotion from the other room gets his attention and he moves fast.

ARTHUR

Rosey sits draped over Dylan. He's trying not to panic in the way he's been shown by his gang leaders, but when it comes to having a gun pushed in your face, it's hard not to lose control. Rosey is casually scrolling through his mobile with one hand, the gun in the other. She holds up the phone and the recording of Jolene Hall confessing to hiring a hitwoman to kill her husband plays out. "No wonder you wanted it so bad," says Rosey, glaring at me.

"Is that the only copy?" I ask, and he nods.

"She's a fucking rich bitch, she can afford to pay what I asked," he spits angrily.

"You're right, and this is a gesture of goodwill," Albert tells him, throwing a neatly banded wad of cash onto his lap. "Leon and Max will assume this matter is settled. If you approach Jolene or attempt to blackmail her again, they won't be so understanding."

"If they come for me, they'll start a war," he spits, grinning.

"Which they are prepared to do. Now, sweet pea, untangle yourself from him. Albert needs to make sure he has the message," I say.

# ARTHUR

Rosey holds out her hand, and I take it, pulling her to me. She takes my arms and wraps them around her, pressing her back to my front and watching as Albert lays into the gang member. She occasionally pushes back with her arse, and I swear she's turned on by the violence.

I remember Meli is in the kitchen and look back over my shoulder to find her watching from the doorway. But her eyes aren't on the bloody mess that is Dylan. Instead, they're watching me and Rosey. When she catches me looking at her, she folds her arms over her chest and forces a smile. "I say we kill him," Rosey announces.

"Good job I'm the boss," I say. "Put your gun away. He lives."

"And if he talks?"

"He won't."

When it looks like the dick is half dead, Albert wipes his hands on his trousers. "That should do it."

Meli doesn't wait a second longer before she leaves. "I think she's mad I brought her," whispers Rosey.

We all head out and down the stairs. Meli is halfway across the car park. I run to catch up with her. "You can't be out here on your own," I snap. My car pulls in, and she stops. "I'll take you both home."

"I can walk," hisses Meli, and I'm not sure why she's suddenly so mad.

"Why is she even here?" I ask, glaring at Rosey.

"I didn't want to stand out. No one goes to a party alone."

"It wasn't part of the plan, Red."

"Speaking of plans, when did you plan on telling me about Jolene dropping us in the shit with her little confession?" asks Rosey.

"No names were mentioned. You didn't need to know."

"Like fuck I didn't. She talked about a hitwoman."

"And you think you're the only one?" I scoff.

"You want me to go after Meli?" Albert asks, and I turn to where Meli is storming off.

"No, I'll fix this. Take Rosey home and remind her how we do business," I snap, marching off after Meli.

"Why are you mad?" I ask after a few minutes of us speed walking in silence.

"Mav is going to lose his mind when I tell him about tonight."

"I know. I'll explain everything."

"What did that guy do to deserve that?" she asks.

"It doesn't matter."

She spins to face me, and we both stop. "It matters to me. If I'm going to witness the beating of a man I helped lure into that place, I want to know what he did."

"Rosey shouldn't have taken you along. It won't happen again." We start walking, but this time slow-

## ARTHUR

er. "I have a bar right around the corner from here. Can I get you a drink to apologise?"

"Are you sure you wouldn't rather take Rosey?" she asks, sounding bitter. It pulls a smile from me—maybe she likes me more than she wants to admit.

"If I wanted to take Rosey, she'd be here instead."

Thankfully, the bar is quiet, with only a few couples talking quietly while the soft music plays a soulful tune. Meli takes a seat by the window, and I order us each a drink and join her. "This isn't like your other bars," she points out.

"It's on the border to E15's streets. I don't put much into it because it'll attract too much attention. I bought it many years ago, before the kids took the streets, but it's one of the first bars I purchased, so I don't want to let it go."

She shrugs out of her jacket and places it on the back of her seat. I can't avoid staring at the lace top she's wearing. It's practically underwear, and if she was mine, she'd definitely not be wearing it out of the bedroom. "You didn't like me touching Rosey," I state. It takes her by surprise, and her brow furrows while she thinks carefully of an answer that won't give her true feelings away.

"Why would I care?" I'm disappointed she didn't find a better comeback.

"You looked annoyed."

"I was annoyed at the situation she'd put me in."

"So, seeing her in my arms didn't bother you?" She shakes her head and takes a sip of her drink. "Okay."

"Okay?" she repeats.

"If you have no objection . . ."

"I don't," she insists. "Go for it."

"I have a question."

"I'm all ears."

"If I was to ask Rosey on a date, what sort of thing is she into?"

Meli's eyes blaze with jealousy, but she forces a smile. "Erm, I'm not sure. She's never really been asked on a date before."

I laugh. "I don't believe that. She's stunning."

Meli inhales sharply. "Maybe dinner and a few drinks," she suggests, ignoring my compliment.

"As a woman, what's your ideal date?"

She thinks, then asks, "No limits or reasonable date ideas?"

I grin. "Try both."

"Okay, reasonable date would be an outdoor movie and dinner somewhere nice. Not a bar kind of meal, but a real restaurant with chandeliers and candles."

I raise my eyebrows. "That's reasonable?" I tease.

"No limits would be a surprise flight to somewhere romantic, maybe Paris, dinner in the Eiffel Tower, followed by a night in an expensive hotel."

# ARTHUR

"A night?" I repeat, laughing again. "Is this a first date?"

She presses her lips together, holding back her smile. "I guess it depends on who the date is with."

"If he was a real gentleman, he wouldn't book a hotel for the first date. It would be too presumptuous."

"I just love the thought of silk sheets, a room overlooking the city." She closes her eyes. "A walk-in shower big enough for two." Her eyes shoot open again, like she didn't mean to say it out loud, and she blushes.

Disappointment seeps in. I can't give her that. Romance and cosy nights in aren't my thing. "You've really thought about it."

"What about you?"

"Men don't dream of dates. They mainly think about the rewards."

She blushes deeper. "Tell me the most romantic date you've been on."

"Easy, a few nights on my boat in the Caribbean. Secluded, romantic, and I had her all to myself for three solid days. I don't think we moved from the bedroom." I smirk. "That's a lie, we moved around the boat doing the same actions that belong in the bedroom."

"Of course, you have a boat," she mutters, rolling her eyes.

# NICOLA JANE

"I sold it. Too many memories."

"Because of the woman?"

"Because I killed her and her lover on it." She gasps, and I take a drink, unsure why I just confessed that to her. Luckily, my mobile begins buzzing in my pocket. I retrieve it and sigh. "It's your brother." I answer, "Mav, she's safe. She's with me."

"What the fuck happened tonight?" he yells. "And why was my sister on the Abbey Road estate?"

"Hasn't Rosey filled you in?"

"All she told me was she was doing her job and no one got hurt, so I should fucking chill." I want to laugh at how laidback Rosey is, but I don't. Instead, I tell him I'll bring Meli home and explain everything.

# Chapter Five

MELI

"Why are you yelling?" I hiss while Mav paces angrily.

"Because they exposed you to a gang full of street rats who'll take any opportunity to make a bit of cash," he yells.

"It's not that deep," mutters Rosey, filing her nails and not looking the least bit sorry. "Newsflash, your sister isn't a child, Mav."

He slams both hands on his desk, leaning forward in a threatening manner. I only got back five minutes ago, and he's not cooled down at all. She raises her eyes to meet his but isn't scared, not even a little. "She's been through a lot," he growls.

I rise to my feet, feeling horrified he'd say that in front of Rosey, who's also dealt with a lot of shit, and Arthur, who knows nothing of my past and I'd like to keep it that way. "You're so out of order," I mutter, heading for the door.

"I'm looking out for you," he yells.

I scoff. "You're years too late, Mav." I hear Rosey's sharp intake of breath as I leave the office. I regret the words as soon as they've left my mouth, but I can't take them back now I've said them. I make my way to the bar because it will be busy and he's less likely to cause a scene there, if he bothers to follow me at all.

Hadley and Rylee are sprawled out on the couch, and I shove my way in between the pair so they have to sit up.

"Who are you hiding from?" asks Hadley.

"Mav," I mutter, folding my arms and slouching back. "He's driving me nuts."

"He wasn't happy with the whole street gang party," Rylee confirms.

"You guys have to help me," I say desperately. "I can't keep living like this. How the hell will I ever meet a man with him constantly watching over my shoulder?"

"He just wants to keep you safe," says Rylee.

"I don't need him to, Rylee. I'm a grown woman!"

## ARTHUR

"Really?" comes Mav's voice from behind me. I groan, sinking lower into the couch. "Because you don't fucking act like it, Amelia."

"God, do you realise how much you sound like Dad right now?" I know those words will hurt him.

He moves around the couch until he's standing in front of me. He's raging, and there's practically steam coming from his ears. "You want to live like a real grown-up, Meli? Be my guest. Cos there's a big wide world out there just waiting for you. Try getting a job instead of living off me and Mum."

Mama B walks over. It's not often she gets involved in our arguments, but I can see that today, she intends to. "Why are you yelling?" she asks Mav.

"Because it's all he does," I snap.

"Meli thinks we're stifling her," he mocks. "She's going to give adulthood a go."

"She's already an adult," Mum replies, clearly confused.

"Really? She lounges around the club doing fuck all, living off the food we all buy, not contributing to any of the bills. So, other than her age, tell me what she does that's adulting," he demands.

Mum looks my way, and I can see her mind working fast to think of something. I stand, ready to fight my own corner. "I look after all the kids," I tell him. "Who do you call for when you need an afternoon fuck with Rylee?" I ask, arching a brow.

"Jesus," mumbles Rylee, covering her face with her hands.

"And who takes care of Oakley when Hadley is at work?"

"Everyone, Meli. Everyone takes care of the kids. No specific adult oversees that because there are always adults around. You just happen to be the one on their level because you've never actually grown the fuck up."

"Come on, guys, that's enough," says Hadley gently.

"Shut up, Hadley," we both say together. She's always been the reasonable one out of the three of us.

Arthur watches from the bar with an amused expression on his face, and my embarrassment dials up a notch. "Maverick, you don't see me as an adult, but that's not my problem, it's yours. I do plenty of adult shit, just ask your brothers."

Maverick's eyes bug out of his head and anger rolls off him. "Grim was the only stupid fucker to break that rule, Meli, and he paid the price. None of my brothers would dare fuck up like that again," he snaps. Hadley stands, and I want to reach out for her and apologise for Mav's insensitive remark, but I also don't want to bring more attention to it, so I let her walk away.

"Well done, big brother, now you've upset Hadley."

# ARTHUR

"You did that the day you had sex with her old man," he mutters.

"They were not together," I hiss through gritted teeth.

"You both need to stop," Mum warns.

"From now on, Meli pays her way," Mav announces. "No more handouts, no more free lodgings."

"She doesn't have a job," Mum argues.

"Then she'd better act like an adult and get one," he says, smirking. "We'll take a cut from her wage like we do everyone's. And Mum, I mean it when I say no more handouts. She doesn't get a penny from you, okay?"

Mum bites her lip, giving me a guilty shrug. "It's fine, Mum, I'll get a job. Maybe I'll get a new place to live too, then I don't have to answer to Dad's mini-me." I march off to the bar, reaching behind to grab a bottle of beer.

Mav's right behind me to take it back. "That shit isn't free anymore, Meli. You get that when you start paying your way."

I growl in frustration and head for the exit, in need of air.

A few minutes pass and Arthur steps out. His hands are in his pockets, and the casual vibe he's got going on is hot. "Do you always fight like that with him?" He still has a smirk on his face.

"I don't like being bossed around."

He sniggers. "I have three brothers to boss around and none of them would dare speak to me like you just spoke to Maverick."

"Sisters are a different species."

"I'm grateful I don't have any." He stands beside me, and we both stare out at nothing in particular, as the car park is pretty much empty and the road outside is quiet. "I can help on the job front. I've cleared it with Maverick."

"Thanks, but no. I can do this on my own." The fact he's already spoken to Mav about it pisses me off. If my brother wants me to be independent, he needs to stop okaying everything that involves me.

"It's just some paperwork, filing, organising my office. Rylee said you're good at it."

"I can find my own job." I turn to go back inside, but Arthur's hand catches my wrist, and my skin tingles under his touch. He still stares ahead as he speaks to me, and I'm reminded of exactly why I can't work for him. I want him too much, and this smouldering charm he's got is off the scale.

"You need a job, and I need an employee. Don't miss an opportunity because you're mad at your brother. I'll send a driver to collect you at ten tomorrow." His eyes slowly run down my body. "Office attire." And I swear, before he releases me, I see heat in his eyes.

# ARTHUR

ARTHUR

I was dubious about allowing Meli to work in close proximity to me, but the chances are I'll be out of the office a lot, and I felt bad for her. Mav practically humiliated her in front of me, an outsider to the club. It's not how he usually behaves, and he apologised, but it didn't stop me wanting to fuck him up for upsetting her. That thought alone scared the shit out of me. I like Mav, and I like what we've created together. We make a lot of money and it's a good partnership, but Meli makes me wanna rip it apart and take care of her forever.

Rosey brings me from thoughts of her friend when she sits beside me. I drag my eyes away from the female dancing in front of me, though I'd hardly noticed her until now. "Fancy seeing you here." Rosey grins, handing me a whiskey. She leans back, relaxing against the leather couch, and watches the female. "Is this what you do to relax?"

"What are you doing here, Red?"

"Albert told me to meet him here."

I also have a meeting with my brother shortly, which is why I'm here in his strip club.

The dancer crawls across the small podium and runs her finger down my tie. "And you thought you'd come into my private area?" I ask, arching my brow.

"I wanted to know what you were doing back here," she says, grinning.

I inhale sharply, closing my eyes when the dancer rakes her nails across my thigh. "You're ruining my dance," I mutter to Rosey.

I feel her hand slide up my other thigh. "I could make it better," she whispers, and my cock twitches. It's the most daring she's been so far with her flirting, and my resolve is hanging on by a thread. I slap my hand over hers, halting it. She laughs, and I feel her shift closer. I've just made myself a challenge for her. "Why are you putting up a fight, Arthur? We both want it." Her breath tickles my ear, and my cock gets harder. I turn my head slightly, and when I open my eyes, the dancer is gone and my lips are almost touching Rosey's.

"Sorry I'm late," says Albert, entering the room and causing my erection to deflate. I smirk at Rosey's annoyed expression and stand, shaking hands with him.

"You're just in time," I say, relief clear in my voice.

---

Our meeting runs smoothly, and I enlist Rosey's help on three more jobs. After an hour, she makes her excuses to leave, something about her kid, which

# ARTHUR

always makes me laugh because of her line of work. She doesn't seem the motherly type.

Albert tops up my glass and signals for a dancer to join us. We've moved into the main room now, but in front of each table, there's a dance podium. "What did I interrupt between you two earlier?" he asks.

I watch the dancer for a moment, mesmerised by her green eyes. "You ever felt torn?" I ask. "Between women?"

He laughs. "Fuck, you're asking me for woman advice?"

"God, no." I scoff because he's terrible at it. "I just keep getting distracted. It's like there's a devil and an angel either side of me, and I want them both."

"Are we talking little devils on the shoulder guiding you or actual females?"

"The latter," I say on a sigh.

"Just don't get distracted, Art. Fuck them both or don't, but keep your head in the game. We've got too much going on to let women get in your head."

---

I arrive at the office before Meli. I don't plan on being here a lot when she's around. What Albert said makes sense, and seeing as I can't just fuck the sister of a business associate, I figure avoidance is key. And

# NICOLA JANE

once I've shown her what I need from her, I'll lay low.

But I'm not prepared for the sight that is work mode Amelia, and when she saunters in wearing the office attire I requested, I about bust a ball. The knee-length tightly-fitted skirt clings to her arse perfectly, and the white blouse is tucked in neatly with the top two buttons open, giving me a slight glimpse of her cleavage. *Fuck, I'm screwed.*

"Good morning." She smiles brightly. "Show me where you want me."

Images of her bent naked over my desk skip through my mind. *Yep, this was a bad idea.* I stand abruptly, and her smile falters. Straightening my jacket, I move over to the piles of paperwork on what will be her desk. "All this," I point it out, "needs filing in date order."

She raises her eyebrows. "Wow, that's a lot of paperwork."

"Recent stuff needs to go in that cabinet," I tell her. "The rest should be archived. Follow me."

I lead her to the next floor, an attic space above my office. It's dusty and dark, and when I turn on the light, she screws her face up in disgust. I point to the shelving along one wall where there are archive boxes in year order. "Each box has a monthly filing system." I pull one down and lift the lid to show her.

# ARTHUR

"I need something comfy to wear if I'm going to be dragging dirty boxes down," she mutters, glancing down at her white shirt.

"I have spare clothes in my office. There might be an old shirt in there you can cover up with." My mobile rings. "I have to take this," I say, spotting Rosey's name. Meli sees it too and her smile fades. I hand her the box and leave her to it.

---

I watch in admiration. Rosey has skills when it comes to taking someone's life, and I'm mesmerised. I've seen death too many times, mainly at the hands of myself or my brothers, but I've never watched a woman kill. The way she lured my target from his office and to the meeting point was effortless, like he was her puppy dog and she had complete control. I glance over at Albert, who looks equally impressed as Rosey sits on the target's lap facing him. She gently brushes the hair from his eyes and smiles sweetly. If I didn't know the truth, I'd think they were lovers.

"Now, let's get down to business," she says, glancing my way. "Mr. Taylor?"

I step forward. "The rules were simple, were they not?"

"Yes," the man mutters. "Mr. Taylor, I'm sorry—"

# NICOLA JANE

Rosey slices his throat. I'm so shocked, I stare open-mouthed, then check to my left, where Albert is staring back at me. "Sorry, I was bored," she says, jumping from the guy's lap and wiping her blade on his shirt. "Is anyone else hungry? I'm starving." She begins to unbutton her blood-stained shirt. "I skipped breakfast for this."

"What the fuck was that?" I eventually ask.

She drops her shirt to the ground and stands before us in a white lace bra, which is also blood stained. "You didn't want him dead?"

"Well, yes, but . . ."

"Then what's the problem?"

"It's not how we do business," Albert states, staring at the gurgling mess before us.

"You hired me to do a job, I did it." She bends and begins to rummage through her rucksack. "I wasn't in the mood for a long, drawn-out thing today. I have Ollie home sick and—"

"Ollie?" Albert repeats, looking at me for an explanation.

"Her kid," I confirm.

"He was up most the night with a fever, and do you think I could get through to the doctor first thing?" She's ranting, seemingly oblivious to the situation. "Of course not. What is the point in having an NHS that we can't access? I'm on the verge of going private." She slides her leggings down her legs

# ARTHUR

and screws them into a ball with her shirt, not fazed by me and Albert staring at her lace underwear. "So, I've had to ask Mama B to watch him, which I know pisses her off. I mean, of course, it would—he's the son of her dead husband. Not that she'd say anything because she's far too nice."

"I'm gonna step out to call clean-up," Albert mutters, shaking his head as he leaves.

"And because you hired Meli, I couldn't ask her," Rosey continues. "But I guess it's the life of a working mu—" I pull her to me and slam my lips against hers. It takes us both by surprise, even more so when I lift her into my arms and she wraps her legs around my waist. I push her against the wall, our mouths locked in a hungry kiss. And then I see Meli's face in my mind. The disappointment in her eyes is crippling, and I freeze. Rosey senses it and pulls back, panting breathlessly. "You're stopping . . . why are you stopping?"

"This . . . I shouldn't . . ." I lower her to the ground. "I don't know what the fuck came over me," I mutter, turning away and adjusting my trousers. "I'm sorry."

"Don't apologise, I'm not complaining."

"You should be. That was out of order. I don't fraternise with my employees."

"Employee?" she repeats, quirking a brow. "I'm nobody's employee." She begins to dress in clean clothes, stuffing her bloodied garments into a plastic bag and then into her rucksack. I remain silent until she's finished. "Right, if you don't need me for anything else, I'll get off."

"You want me to drop you home?"

She scoffs, shaking her head. "No."

I watch her leave and feel a sense of relief. I guess Meli is who I crave, but why the fuck did I have to kiss her best friend to figure that shit out?

# Chapter Six

MELI

I got started the second Arthur left the office. I sorted some of the paperwork into year order, then into month order, and now, I'm sat in the middle of the floor, surrounded by paperwork and feeling totally out of my depth. Not because I don't know how to file, but because this is taking forever and I'm not even a quarter of the way through the piles. I flop back and stare up at the ceiling. Damn Maverick and his stupid authority.

"Am I paying you to lounge around?" I sit up quickly, hurting my neck. Arthur is staring down at me, looking annoyed.

"Sorry, I was taking a minute."

# NICOLA JANE

"Nice shirt. Did you have to take your clothes off to wear it?" he asks, arching a brow as he steps over the piles to get to his desk. I glance down at the light pink Armani shirt I chose from his wardrobe. There was nothing old-looking but just a lot of expensive white shirts. At least I chose a non-white item. He sits in his office chair and rubs at his tired face.

"Well . . . yeah, I didn't want to ruin my stuff, and that skirt was a little restrictive for climbing and hauling boxes around," I say. "Everything okay, boss?" I ask.

"Boss?" he repeats before adding a small laugh.

"I wasn't sure how to address you now that I work for you." I pick up the next pile and begin to skim through it.

"Mr. Taylor is fine when people are around. Otherwise, Arthur."

"How's Rosey?" I ask.

He uncovers his face and glares at me. "What?"

"I assume you met her. She called before you left . . ." I trail off because whatever I've said has pissed him off further. "Never mind."

"Don't assume anything, and my working relationship with Rosey is nothing to do with you. I know she's your friend, but I like to keep my work life and private life separate, so I won't discuss our working relationship with you."

# ARTHUR

"Okayyyy," I say, dragging it out. "Sorry I asked." I gather the oldest pile of paperwork and stand before making my way upstairs to the archives. Maybe Arthur needs some alone time.

I spend an hour filing the pile before returning back to the office. I'm surprised to find Rosey and Arthur in what looks to be a deep conversation. I cough to make myself known, and Rosey spins to face me. She's flushed and her smile falters when she sees me. "Hey," she says, "I got you lunch." She points to the paper bag on my desk. "Mama B said you forgot it."

I peek into the bag and scrunch my nose up. "Yeah, I didn't fancy it. I was hoping she wouldn't notice."

"You look like you've worked hard," she comments, smirking. I glance down at the now dirty shirt and matching hands. "Should office work be so dirty?"

"It's not what I was expecting," I say with a laugh.

Arthur stands abruptly. "Take your lunch break, Amelia." And then he leaves. I turn back to Rosey, who stares after him.

"Everything okay?" I ask.

"Yeah, why wouldn't it be?" I shrug, and she comes closer, taking a seat at my desk. "We kissed," she blurts out like she didn't mean to but couldn't help it.

I stare wide-eyed. "Oh."

## NICOLA JANE

"Oh?" she repeats. "That's all you have?"

I don't know what else to say. My heart hurts, and I don't understand why because there's nothing between Arthur and me. And now they've kissed, there never can be. "I'm just surprised. I didn't put you two together."

"Meli, we kissed, we didn't get married. Seriously, since when did you start believing in happy ever after?"

"But you like him. You said you liked him, so I'm just assuming he feels the same?" I ask in the hope she'll answer.

"Probably," she says, shrugging. "He plays his cards close to his chest, but who wouldn't like me, right?" She laughs, and I join her. I have to be happy for her—she's my best friend, and she deserves this.

---

The rest of the afternoon passes in a haze of papers and dust. Arthur doesn't reappear, and I work much faster with no distraction. It's almost five when the office door opens and Maverick comes in. We haven't spoken since we argued, so I'm shocked to see him. He holds up a spare bike helmet. "Came to take you home," he mutters.

"I can walk."

# ARTHUR

He sighs. "Look, Meli, I don't like fighting with you. This is my way of making up."

I take the helmet, and he smiles a little. "Fancy a burger on the way back?" I smile too. We never spend any time together alone. I nod, and he relaxes. "Great. Let's go."

---

We order as soon as we arrive. I skipped Mum's lunch, so I'm hungry, tucking right into the burger and fries. Maverick watches in amusement. "Mama B make you lunch?"

"Tuna," I say, rolling my eyes.

He grins. "She's from the days where they made a packed lunch for work instead of buying a meal deal."

"I was busy anyway. I didn't stop to eat."

"Did you have a good first day?" he asks, and I nod, taking another bite of the burger. "I'm sorry for what I said to you. I didn't mean to lose it the way I did."

I shrug it off. "It's fine. You were right. It's time I got a job and started thinking of my future."

"Wow, one day at work and you have a future planned?" he teases.

I smile. "I've never had to think about it. Or never wanted to, I'm not sure which. But I know this is the first step, and it felt good today. I had a purpose to get out of bed and do something other than hang around the club and look after the kids."

"And Arthur, what's he like to work for?"

I laugh. "He's grumpy, busy, and hardly in the office, so it's fine. Although Rosey stopped by. I think she and him have something going."

"Oh?"

"Yeah, I think Rosey likes him."

"Well, they're suited to one another. Crazy and the beast," he jokes. My heart twists again. Everyone sees it, they're perfect for one another.

"They are," I mutter. "I hope he works out for her. She deserves it."

"And you?"

I look up, my eyes wide with panic. "Me?" I ask.

"Yeah, are you gonna find someone and settle down? Is that part of your future plans?"

"I'm in no rush," I mutter, lowering my eyes to my empty plate. "And you don't exactly make it easy."

He nods. "I know. Rylee had words with me." He laughs. "I'll try and back off. I just . . . with everything that happened, I wanna protect you."

"I know. I'm lucky to have you."

ARTHUR

"It's not like you," says Albert.

I knock back the whiskey and wince. "What?"

# ARTHUR

"Drinking like this. You hate drinking that shit. What's wrong?"

"Who said there was anything wrong? Maybe for one night, I fancy letting go, forgetting about everything and getting wasted."

"You've always said you shouldn't let go because that's when you're vulnerable."

I groan, slamming my glass down. He's like a fun sponge sucking out the light. "You're right. I'll go back to running the family, keeping every fucker safe, and letting this fucking world suck the life outta me."

He sits beside me at the bar. "Start talking."

"Is it so wrong that I want one night off?"

"Is it a woman? Is it about what you said the other day, with the angel and demon on your shoulder?"

"I came close to giving in," I confess. "The demon was right there for the taking, and I lost control for a second. I never do that."

"I'm assuming the demon is a woman or this is really weird."

"I just don't understand, Albert. I'm around women all the goddamn time and I don't care. I don't notice. I can fuck any one of them and never see them again and I don't give a shit. But with these two, I want them both for very different reasons. And why? I've never thought about settling down and . . ." I realise I've said too much, and Albert is staring at me like I have two heads.

"You wanna settle down?"

"I didn't think I did, until now. Maybe I'm ready."

"How the fuck is a wife gonna fit in to what we do, Art? Think about it. When you're gone all night or when you're home covered in blood, no sane woman would put up with it."

"Who said sane?" I smirk, finishing my drink and thinking about Rosey. She'd definitely fit into my life. And then there's Meli not quite as insane as her friend, but she'd get this life, no question.

"You wanna know what I think?"

"No."

"You need to get on with business. Take your mind off both women and fuck a random. Then tomorrow, focus on making us rich. It's what you do best."

"Why do you have to talk sense?" I grumble.

"It's my job—talk sense and keep you on track. Are we good?" he asks.

I nod, holding up my glass. "I'm just gonna have one more."

---

I'm seeing double. I hate feeling like this, and I'm pissed at myself for drinking so much as I fall into my chair. The red-head I picked up falls on top of

# ARTHUR

me, giggling as she lifts her skirt. She sinks down onto my erection. Fuck knows how I even got it up, and I don't remember getting it out of my trousers. She groans, digging her nails into my shoulders. "Condom," I murmur, opening my desk drawer and reaching for one. She slams her mouth over mine and moves faster. "Stop," I whisper.

"No chance," she pants.

My head falls back against the chair and I close my eyes. I need to sleep.

---

"Holy fucking shit." The voice is loud, and my head aches. I squint, letting some light into my eyes. "Are you kidding me?" The voice is louder now, and it belongs to Albert.

"Who the hell are you?" It's another voice, this one female.

"You don't remember me?" he asks.

"Aren't you one of Arthur's security?"

"I'm his brother, and there better be a damn good reason why he's passed out and you're naked."

"Oh Lord, what the hell have I walked in on?" That voice belongs to Meli, and I immediately open my eyes fully to discover I'm in my office. I look down. I'm naked, and to my side is Jolene Hall.

## NICOLA JANE

"*Jolene Hall*," I say out loud, my words laced in surprise and shock. "Fuck . . . what the fuck?"

"Indeed," says Albert, arching his brows in judgement.

Jolene looks sheepish as she sits, grabbing her dress from the floor and pulling it on. "I should go."

"Not so fast, princess," snaps Albert. "I have a few questions. Like did you use protection?" He glares at me, and I suddenly feel like a kid under his dad's angry scrutiny. I'm also aware that Meli is still staring wide-eyed at this whole shitshow.

"You wanna do this later, when I'm awake properly and dressed maybe?" I ask.

"You want her to walk out of here not knowing if she could get pregnant, brother?" he snaps. "Cos I ain't gonna sleep well knowing she might become a part of this family."

"Rude," mutters Jolene, slipping on her shoes. "And, of course, we did."

"Cos I'm gonna believe anything you say," Albert utters, rolling his eyes.

"It's not like your brother can remember, is it?" She sneers, smirking my way.

I sigh heavily. "Get her the pill."

"What pill?" she asks, looking alarmed.

Albert goes to the safe and punches in the number. "We're out," he declares, slamming it closed angrily. He turns to Meli. "Go to the chemist. It's at the end

# ARTHUR

of the road. I need the morning-after pill." He pulls some cash from his wallet and holds it out for her to take, but she stares at it with distain.

"No."

Albert frowns. "Excuse me?"

"I said no. If she wants to take that pill, she can get it."

"Which I don't," Jolene chimes in.

"Of course, you don't. Who wouldn't want to tie down Arthur Taylor? But it's not happening, sweetheart, not on my watch," growls Albert. "You're hired to do a job, so do it," he adds, glaring at Meli.

She stares at me for a moment, perhaps wanting me to cut in, but I don't. My head hurts, I feel like shit, and I really don't want to have a kid with Jolene Hall. "Do it, Amelia," I order. I don't miss the disappointment in her eyes as she snatches the cash and leaves, muttering words under her breath which I don't quite catch but I'm certain aren't good.

"I'm not taking your little pill," Jolene says, grabbing her bag and heading for the door. "You can't make me."

Albert grabs her arm and hauls her back, practically throwing her onto the couch. "Watch me."

She looks nervously around the office. There's no escape. Albert is way too fast. "My brothers will hear about this."

"Sweetheart, I'm not scared of anyone, least of all your chuckle brothers. The best thing for you . . . and them . . . is to take this pill and keep the fuck away from my brother."

I groan loudly, rubbing my face harder. "Jesus, Albert, give it a rest. She'll take the pill. Ease up."

He scoffs angrily. "Ease up? Imagine what our life would be like if I did."

"Imagine how less stressed you'd feel," I counter.

"And how many fuck-ups you'd continue to make."

I stand, squaring my shoulders. He might be my right-hand man, but he isn't the head of this family. That's solely on me. "Remember who the fuck I am," I snarl.

"I should leave," mutters Jolene, standing again. This time, it's me who pushes her back to sitting, and she visibly swallows.

"You'll take the damn pill because you don't want to be tied to me. I'm not a good man." I turn back to Albert. "And you need to take a step back, maybe get your dick sucked for once, and remember who's in charge. Because you might stand tall by my side, but I put you there and I can easily put you down."

Meli comes back and stops dead, catching us in a staredown. She places the pill packet on the table and hands a bottle of water to Jolene. "Have you taken it before?" she asks her, completely ignoring the tension in the room. Jolene takes the packet, nodding.

# Chapter Seven

MELI

I can't help feeling annoyed. Jolene took the pill and left, but not before Albert forced her to open her mouth and show she'd actually swallowed it. Who the hell does that? Then Albert left without another word to Arthur. I missed the argument between them, but the tension was enough to chill me. And now, Arthur is in the room next to his office, taking a shower and humming to himself like everything is fine. But it isn't fine. He had sex with Jolene Hall in his office. An office I have to sit in. And then there's the whole thing he's got going on with Rosey. He kissed her just yesterday, and now, he's having sex with random people. Poor Rosey.

# ARTHUR

I sit at my desk. I've finally managed to clear enough paperwork to be able to work at it. The postman knocks on the office door, smiling when he sees me. I met him yesterday, and he's the loveliest postman I've ever met. Once I told him I was the new office girl, he insisted he'd bring the mail up to the office rather than leave it at the bar downstairs. "Good morning, Meli. How's your second day going?" He hands me the mail, and I laugh.

"You want the truth or a lie?"

"Sounds interesting, so definitely the truth."

"I've already had to go way above my duties. I've also seen my boss naked, and I've witnessed an argument between two dangerous men. What about you?"

He laughs too. "Wow. Busy morning and it's not even ten. The naked boss, was that something you chose to see?"

I shake my head. "Nope. And he wasn't in my bed, which makes it super weird for you to understand, but I won't scare you with the details."

Arthur comes into the office fastening his cufflinks to the crisp white shirt he's now wearing coupled with grey suit trousers. "Good morning. Is there a reason you're up here?" he asks, bringing his steely blue eyes to the postman.

"I asked him to bring me the mail so I can file it directly rather than have you throw it on a pile somewhere," I say. The postman gives me an awkward smile and turns to leave. "Thanks again. See you tomorrow."

"Have a good rest of the day, Meli," he replies before disappearing back downstairs.

"I'm not sure how long I've been here, and I've never made friends with the postman," he remarks, sitting at his desk. I set about opening the letters and checking them for importance. I feel Arthur's eyes burning into me. "You're not speaking to me?" He sounds amused.

I collect the letters Arthur needs to look at and take them to his desk. "I don't appreciate having to run out first thing to clear up your mess," I say. "And please remember that Rosey is my friend."

I go to turn away, but he grabs my wrist. "What's that got to do with anything?"

"Yesterday you were kissing her, and today, I find you naked with Jolene. I don't want Rosey to get hurt. She doesn't deserve that."

He rises to his feet and towers over me. "She told you?"

"Like I said, we're friends."

"Is that the real reason you're mad with me, Meli?" he asks, his voice almost a whisper. He uses his free hand to sweep my hair from my cheek and tuck it behind my ear. "Or was it seeing me naked with another woman?"

# ARTHUR

I almost roll my eyes at his ego trip. "I have to tell Rosey about today."

"Of course. There's nothing between us, so she won't be upset."

"You sound confident. I hope you're right."

"But you, Meli, you look upset."

I force myself to remain calm despite my heart beating out of my chest. Being so close, feeling his touch, it makes me wonder what it feels like to kiss him, to be held by him . . . to be that woman to wake up beside him after a night filled with pleasure. Instead, I take a step back. "I have work to do."

---

At lunchtime, Hadley appears at the office door with Oakley. "We thought you'd like to grab lunch," she explains. It's been a long time since Hadley and I did anything together that wasn't family related. It warms my heart she actually thought of me.

I wrap Oakley in a hug, despite only seeing her this morning. "You always know exactly what I need," I reply, grabbing my bag. Arthur left an hour ago. After our earlier exchange, we didn't speak another word.

We go to a nearby sandwich bar, and once we've ordered, we find a seat by the window and Hadley gives Oakley the iPad to keep her occupied. "So, how's work?" she asks, then laughs. "It feels strange asking you that."

"I like it. I'm not doing much other than filing at the minute, but it's nice to be out of the club and doing my own thing."

"Yeah, you look happier."

"Mav came to see me last night. He apologised for yelling at me."

"He said he would." They're much closer out of the three of us, and sometimes, that stings. It wasn't like this before I fucked everything up.

"They still haven't announced Rylee's pregnancy," I say. "Did she say when they would?"

Hadley shakes her head. "Mav is really excited, though. It's sweet to see him like that."

"He told you?" Rylee told the girls a month back, but we were sworn to secrecy because Maverick didn't want her to tell anyone until she was at least twelve weeks. Hadley realises what she's let slip and winces. "It's fine," I rush to reassure her. "Of course, he'd tell you, you're close. It's good he's got someone to talk to."

She reaches over the table and rubs my hand. "Sorry, Meli. I didn't mean to be so inconsiderate. He just needed to tell someone, yah know? It's his first kid, so he's gonna be excited."

I nod, swallowing the lump in my throat. "Of course."

# ARTHUR

She bites her lower lip, a guilty expression all over her face. "Anyway, how are you and Arthur getting on?" She wiggles her brows suggestively, and I appreciate her changing the subject, even if it is about that arse.

"He's a good boss. I don't really see him," I mutter. My heart hurts too much to entertain her with stories of Arthur and his antics this morning.

"Did you speak to Rosey about how you feel?"

"Why would I?" I ask.

"Well, because you like him and she's not that into him."

"Actually, I think she is. She got there first, Hadley, and I'm okay with that."

"But Rosey just wants . . ." She glances at her daughter to check she isn't watching before mouthing the word 'sex'. "And you like him, like him."

"Stop," I mutter. "We're not in school. They're suited and perfect for each other. I want them to work out. He's my boss, and I don't see him as anything else."

Our food arrives and I use the break in conversation to change the subject onto her work as a solicitor, something she loves to talk about, and she's soon giving me the rundown on an important case she's taken on.

# NICOLA JANE

When I get back to the office, I head straight for the bathroom. I drop my bag on the floor and grip the edge of the counter, staring at myself in the mirror. I hate myself. I really hate myself. Tears fill my eyes, and the longer I stare at my reflection, the angrier I am. "Why would Maverick talk to you when you're a fucking cheating, bitch? They all hate you. They put up with you because they have no choice, but they hate you," I spit the words. "You're disgusting. No one could ever love you."

I slam my hand against my reflection hard and the mirror cracks. I cry out, hitting it again until I feel a sharp pain in the palm of my hand. I fall back against the wall and slide down until my backside hits the floor, and then I sob into my bloody palm.

The door opens and I push up to stand quickly, wiping my face. Arthur fills the doorway, and when his eyes land on me, his brow furrows with concern. "What happened?" he asks, grabbing my wrist and staring at the blood in my hand. "Did someone hurt you?"

I use my other hand to continue to wipe my wet cheeks, shaking my head and forcing a laugh. "No, nothing like that. I fell . . . against the mirror. I, erm, well, I cut my hand, but I'm fine and I'll pay for the damage."

He turns his head to check out the cracked mirror and his frown deepens. "Fell?" he repeats sceptically.

# ARTHUR

I nod, and even though his expression tells me he doesn't believe me, he nods too and swoops down to collect my bag from the floor. "Okay, let's clean this up."

He sits me at his desk. His office chair is huge and swallows me, but it's comfy. He opens his desk drawer and retrieves a first aid kit. I spy the gun beside it, but he closes the drawer quickly and takes my hand again. "You went to lunch with Hadley," he says, and I glance up at the office camera blinking from the corner of the room. It's connected to his mobile, so it makes sense he sees what goes on when he's away.

"Yes."

"What did she say to upset you?"

"I'm not upset," I lie, and he laughs to himself, shaking his head.

"Yah know, lies bother me more than anything else."

"Which is why you should tell Rosey about Jolene."

He wipes my cut with an antiseptic wipe. "If Rosey was to ask, of course, I'd tell her, but I don't know why she would, seeing as there's nothing between us."

"Nothing?" I ask, arching a brow.

He smirks. "There's attraction, Meli. What hot-blooded male wouldn't find her attractive? But hot, raw fucking isn't a relationship."

# NICOLA JANE

"Hot, raw . . ." I repeat, my heart racing. "You slept with Rosey?" I don't know why the words sound shaky as they leave my mouth.

Arthur wraps a bandage around my hand and ties it off. "You sound upset again."

I open and close my mouth a few times, unable to find the right words. I am upset. I just don't know why, or at least, I don't want to admit it, not even to myself. "She just didn't tell me."

He smiles, placing a hand either side of the chair. He moves his face closer to mine, and I hold my breath, wondering if he's about to kiss me or call me out on my bullshit lie. "I haven't had sex with Rosey." He pushes off the chair and turns his back, cleaning away the first aid kit.

I release the breath and stare down at the bandage. "I feel like an outsider," I whisper, and he stills, keeping his back to me but clearly listening. "At the club. Since I did what I did, I hate myself."

"You mean since Grim?"

"Yes. I regret it, and I hate the way it's put a wedge between myself and Hadley. And I get it, I totally deserve everything and more. They don't intentionally push me out, it just happens. But I feel like I don't belong there anymore."

"Where do you belong?" he asks, turning to face me and leaning against the desk.

# ARTHUR

I shrug. "I don't know that either. Hadley and Maverick share secrets and talk. They hang out. They're close, and I'm happy for them, I am, but..."

"But it reminds you of how you and Hadley used to be." I nod and a tear escapes, sliding down my cheek. "Do they know how you feel?"

"No. Why would I tell them? So I can be the victim? I deserve to feel like this. What I did was unforgivable."

"What you *and* Grim did. You didn't do it alone. And it was years ago. They're together and happy." He uses his thumb to wipe my tears. "Seems like you're punishing yourself for something they don't even think about anymore."

Albert comes in, and Arthur turns away, giving me a moment to compose myself. "You in a better mood?" Arthur asks him.

"I was wrong about what I said yesterday," says Albert. "Forget fucking around. Find the angel, or the devil, and settle the fuck down. We don't need mistakes like Jolene Hall coming back to bite us."

ARTHUR

"We're still not over that?" I ask, smirking.

"Since when do you break your own rule, Art? Sleeping with her could cause all kinds of problems. Not only that, but you went in bareback?"

Meli makes her way over to her desk, and Albert gives her a curious glance. I shake my head, warning him not to say anything to her. She's fragile right now, and if I hadn't fought with my brother earlier, I'd have asked him to leave us so we could continue the conversation. She was opening up to me. One thing's for certain—she smashed her hand into that mirror on purpose, and that worries me. "I couldn't tell you what happened last night, Bert. I was blind drunk, which is why I stayed here and didn't make it home. But glad you noticed I was gone. Imagine if our enemies had gotten to me," I say sarcastically.

"I sent Tommy to check on you, smart arse. He told me you were propping up the bar, and you told him to go home and stop treating you like a fucking kid."

"And yet here you are," I say dryly. "Angel," I turn to Meli, and she looks up from her work. "Could you go check on last night's numbers, please?" She nods and disappears downstairs to find the bar manager.

"Angel?" Albert repeats, grinning like the cat that got the cream. "She's your angel?"

"If you have nothing to do, I can send you on some collections." I know how much he hates that work and thinks it's beneath him.

"That must make Rosey your devil," he says, gasping in mock horror. "Best friends? You dog."

# ARTHUR

"Enough. You're reading way too much into it. Go do some work."

"I guess she's got form," he adds. When I don't respond, he heads for the door. "Didn't Meli fuck her sister's man too?" He stops, and I know by the expression on his face, she's coming up the stairs and she's heard him. He waits for her to step back into the office before making his own escape. I inwardly groan. She didn't need to hear that right now.

Meli hands me the signing-in book. "Sorry about him," I mutter. "He went to the 'how to be an insensitive prick' school."

She raises half a smile. "I've heard worse said about me."

"Meli, you really—"

"I overshared before," she cuts in, halting me mid-sentence. "It won't happen again. You're my boss, and I appreciate you checking up on me, but I'm fine. It was a moment of madness. I'm sorry for off-loading, and I'd appreciate you keeping it to yourself." She gathers a pile of paperwork and heads up to the archives.

# Chapter Eight

MELI

I bang on Rosey's bedroom door. "Get ready," I tell her through the wood. "We're going out."

She pulls the door open and frowns. "What?"

"Get ready. I want to go out, and you're my best friend, so you have to oblige."

She takes the wine bottle from my hand. "Fine by me, come on in."

I drop down on her bed and watch as she begins to pull clothes from her wardrobe. I opted for jeans and a cute low-cut top. Not that I have much cleavage to display, but I'm on a mission to forget Arthur Taylor. She passes me the wine back, and I unscrew the cap and drink right from the bottle. "Bad day?" she asks, settling on a skirt.

# ARTHUR

"Something like that." I sigh heavily. "Listen, I have to tell you something, and I feel really bad, but I can't keep it a secret from you. How serious are you about Arthur?"

She pauses, giving me a suspicious stare, and I know it's because she suspects I've made a move on him. Even my best friend doesn't trust me around her man. "Why?"

"Because I don't think he's worth your time. You deserve better."

"You're talking in riddles, Meli, what's wrong?"

"I saw him with another woman," I tell her, wincing.

She breathes a sigh of relief. "Right, so?"

"I thought you kissed?"

"We're not in school, Meli. He can do what he wants unless we're official, which we're not. *Yet.*"

With that last word lingering in my mind, I drink more wine.

---

The heavy day is weighing me down, and the only thing making me happy right now is shots. "Another four, please," I tell the barman.

"I know you said you had a bad day, Meli, but seriously, it's only Thursday. Slow down."

# NICOLA JANE

"It's like they'll never forgive me," I continue my conversation like she didn't just speak. "How long are they gonna punish me for?"

"Maybe they're not punishing you," Rosey replies, taking the shots and carrying them over to a nearby table. She looks around, and I know she's hoping to see Arthur. "Maybe they're just closer these days."

"He told her about the baby," I repeat.

"You already told me," she says, rolling her eyes. "He can talk to who he wants. Besides, you got rid of a baby, so maybe he thinks it'll upset you."

"What, like I won't be happy for my brother to have his first child? I was happy when Hadley had Oakley, and that was after the whole mess of Grim and me."

"But you weren't exactly happy when she announced it. Perhaps Mav doesn't want you to ruin his announcement too." She laughs, and I narrow my eyes. "Look, I honestly think this is in your head. You're the only one punishing yourself by seeing things that aren't there."

"I need a man," I announce, and she laughs at my dramatics. "If I show I've moved on, they'll be normal around me."

"There's a couple of guys over there who keep looking over."

I glance to my left and see the two guys she's referring to. Both are nice-looking and well dressed.

# ARTHUR

"Smile," I tell her. "You look like you want to murder them." She smiles awkwardly, and I kick her under the table. "Don't fuck this up for me, Rosey. We're not all blessed with a mafia god making moves on us."

It doesn't take long for the two men to come over and introduce themselves as Elijah and Henry. Both work in law and are enjoying a few drinks after work to unwind. I pick off Elijah, mainly because he's giving me all the signals and I like his green eyes. Henry and Rosey head off to the bar, and I seize the moment. After all, that's what I'm vowing to do, or I might be single forever. I grab him by the tie and tug him closer. "You're definitely single?" I ask for the third time.

He grins, his lips only a breath from my own. "I promise." I close the gap as my lips press against his.

ARTHUR

"I got a question," says Tommy, leaning back in the booth and grinning like an idiot. "Fuck, marry, avoid? Rosey, Meli, and Jolene."

Albert almost chokes laughing, spitting his drink down his chin. He wipes it, smirking at me glaring in his direction. "You told them?"

"We're brothers—there are no secrets," he replies, shrugging.

"Fuck Rosey, marry Meli, and avoid Jolene at all costs," answers Charlie. Tommy nods in agreement.

"Why marry Meli? Rosey would be much more fun to tame," Albert argues.

"Grow up," I tell them, knocking back my glass of water. My head is still aching from last night's session, and there's no way I'm repeating that.

"Speak of the angel," says Albert, nodding his head. I look in that direction. "Isn't that her acting like a horny little devil?"

My smile fades at the sight of Meli practically mounting some guy while they eat each other's face off. I stand abruptly, and my brothers fall silent, watching me warily for my next move. They're so in tune with me, they can sense my anger, but as I make my way over, I'm intercepted by Rosey, who places her hands on my chest and smiles seductively. "You haven't called."

I glare at her in annoyance. "Are you responsible for Meli getting in a state?" I snap.

She looks back at her friend and grins. "She said she wanted to get wasted. What kind of friend would I be to stand in the way?"

"Who is he?"

She shrugs. "I have no idea, but he's gorgeous, and I think his luck is in tonight."

I take her by the shoulders and move her to one side, so she's no longer in my way, and I continue

# ARTHUR

towards Meli. I place my hands under her arms and lift her from the guy. She cries out in surprise, and when I place her on the floor, she glares at me angrily. "What the fuck?" she screams.

"Exactly what I was gonna say to you."

"No," she hisses, wagging her finger at me. "You're not doing this to me tonight. Mav is easing up on me, and I am allowed to meet guys."

"Not on my watch." I grab her wrist, noting she's still wearing the bandage on her hand. I begin to pull her away from the bewildered-looking man.

"I'll scream," she warns.

"Be my guest," I say, rolling my eyes. This is my club, and no one comes here without knowing the kind of men who hang out here. Men who won't bat an eyelid to a woman screaming.

"Arthur, I mean it," she says through gritted teeth. And then she begins to scream. A few people turn to see what the commotion is, and two of my security guys look over. I hold a hand up to let them know I've got it, then I pull her against me and cover her mouth.

"Stop, Amelia, or I'll give you a reason to scream." Rosey falls into step beside us.

"Should I take her home?" she asks.

"No. I'll arrange a car to take you. I haven't finished with Meli."

"What does that mean?" she asks.

## NICOLA JANE

"Albert, take Rosey home," I shout over to him, then I turn back to her. "It means exactly what I said, now go." She's torn. I can see it in her face as she watches me drag her friend towards the roof exit.

### MELI

I kick all the way up the stairs to the roof space. He struggles to get me through the door, and when he does, he releases me and I run, putting distance between us. He slams the door closed and leans against it, glaring at me. "Who was that guy?" he asks.

"I have no fucking idea," I yell angrily. "And I didn't get chance to find out, thanks to you. I scream again, stamping my foot in frustration. "You fucking bastard men, you keep fucking up my life." The emotions from the day catch up with me and I ball my fists by my side. "How can I grow up when none of you let me?"

"Get it out," he says calmly. "Scream, shout, tell me exactly how you feel. Get it out, Meli."

"You don't want to know how I feel," I cry. I rub my chest, as it feels tight, and I begin to pace. "You don't care."

"I do," he tells me.

"You?" I ask, almost laughing through my tears. "Arthur Taylor cares about me, the home wrecking whore?"

"Don't say that about yourself," he mutters.

# ARTHUR

I take a few shuddering breaths, unable to calm myself. "You should go after Rosey," I whisper.

"You need me."

"I don't," I cry. "I don't need anyone."

"You're derailing, Meli. I'm not gonna let you fall." I want to scream in his face at how blind he is. I derailed years ago. I've already fallen. And no one was there to catch me.

It begins to rain, but he doesn't budge from blocking the door. "You might not see it now, but I saved you from making a bad decision tonight," he continues. "You would have woken tomorrow full of regret."

I laugh, turning my back on him. "You have no idea how badly I wanted to make bad decisions tonight. It's what it was all about, and regret is my middle name."

"Sleeping with him wouldn't have made you feel better."

I walk to the edge and look down at the people below running for shelter as the rain pours harder. "Don't act like you know me, Arthur. Sex makes me feel good. Men use women all the damn time. You did it to Jolene, so why can't I do the same?"

I feel him behind me, and he places his jacket over my shoulders. He joins me, looking down at the crowds. "You're holding it all in, and you go on these drunken nights to ease the ache in your heart. But it doesn't help, Meli. You know it doesn't. Fucking a nameless, faceless guy who runs out on you first thing . . . you deserve better."

"I don't," I whisper. "I deserve everything I get." I feel him watching me, but I continue to stare below. "I get used because it's all I'm worth. Men look at me and see nothing. Nothing worth anything. Men don't marry girls like me, they use me. I'm the dirty secret. The party girl who's good for a quick fuck in an alley but not good enough to take home to meet mummy."

"Jesus, Meli, why are you talking like that?"

"You wanted the truth, right?" I ask, glancing at him. The rain has soaked his shirt to his skin and his hair is flat to his head. The water runs down his face, dripping from his chiselled chin. "You said I should let it all out."

He turns me to face him and brushes my wet hair from my face. "I don't know who told you that bullshit, but they're wrong. You're perfect, Meli. In every single way."

More tears leave my eyes, mixing with the rain. "You wouldn't say that if you knew the truth."

"Nothing will change my mind." He cups my face in his hands. "You're perfect."

I begin to cry harder. "Stop saying that."

"Perfect," he repeats, forcing me to look at him. "No one comes close." He kisses my nose gently,

# ARTHUR

then my forehead, then my cheek. I hold my breath, staring into his eyes between each chaste kiss. "Perfect. My perfect angel." He gently presses his lips to mine and leaves them there for a second, not breaking our eye contact. "Say it," he whispers against my mouth. I shake my head, and he kisses me again, lingering a little longer. "Meli, say it."

"I can't."

"My perfect angel, say it."

I take another shuddering breath. "Your perfect angel," I whisper, wanting desperately to believe his words. But I don't. I never will.

He smiles, I like that I've made him happy. He's breathing faster, and I sense he's fighting an internal battle. His hand slides to the back of my head, and this time, when he kisses me, he doesn't pull back. He takes it deeper, tilting my head slightly and sweeping his tongue into my mouth. A small moan leaves me, and he kisses me harder, backing me against the ledge. He lifts me to sit there and breaks the kiss to pull my wet top over my head. He drops it on the floor and slides my bra strap down my arm, uncovering my breast. He wastes no time taking me into his mouth. I run my fingers through his wet hair and let my head fall back in pleasure. Feeling his hands unbuttoning my jeans, I lift slightly so he can slide them down my legs. His mouth comes back to my breast. "Trust me?" he asks, and I nod. He gently pushes me to lie back on the ledge. It's wide enough that my body fits, but my head hangs over the edge. I stare at the buildings, now upside down, and wonder if anyone is watching as Arthur runs kisses down my stomach. He peels my underwear away and spreads my legs.

There's a nagging voice somewhere in the back of my mind telling me I should stop this before it goes too far. Arthur is my boss. My best friend likes him, and here I am again, naked and desperate for attention . . . again. Tears leak, dripping from the corners of my eyes and into my hair, but then his mouth is there, buried between my legs, and I cry out in surprise, grabbing onto the edge of the wall and stiffening as he licks and sucks me. He's good, too good, and I'm coming apart in minutes, crying out until my throat is sore. *Why does he have to be so good at what he's doing?*

ARTHUR

I want to fuck her. Right here in the rain, with her hanging over the ledge. I want to bury myself so deep inside her, we're practically joined. But instead, I pull her underwear back into place and take her hands, tugging her to sit up. She looks confused. "You're soaked to the skin," I say, picking her wet top up from the floor. It's too wet to put back on, so I wrap my jacket around her and fasten the buttons.

# ARTHUR

"And you're drunk and upset. I'm taking you home." I rush the words out before I change my mind because, fuck, I really want to. I've never made sensible decisions over what I want before now, and it doesn't feel as good as I thought it would.

"No," she replies, equally as quick. "I don't want to go home right now. I'll make my way to a hotel." She jumps down from the wall and tries to take her top from me, but I hold it tight.

"I'll drive you myself."

We take the stairs all the way down to the private car park in the basement. I open the car door for her, and she slides inside. "I'll get your leather interior wet," she mutters as I climb into the driver's side.

"It's fine."

I drive the fifteen minutes it takes to get to my house. I never invite anyone back here, but I want her here. I want to see her in my home. "This isn't a hotel," she says as the electric gates slide open and I drive in.

She leans forward to take in the large white house with floor-to-ceiling windows. "I had it built," I tell her. "It's the exact image I had in my mind when I sat with the designer. My dream home."

"It's beautiful."

I rush to open her car door and take her hand as she steps out. "Why are we here?" she asks, and for a second, I see worry in her eyes.

# NICOLA JANE

"I don't want anything from you," I reassure her. "You didn't want to go home, and I want to make sure you're safe . . . and dry." I smile, hoping she'll relax. "Or I can take you where you want to go."

She shakes her head. "Here's fine."

We go inside, and I hear her gasp as she looks around in awe at the huge hallway. Rooms lead off through large white double doors, and in the centre is a winding staircase. I kick off my shoes, and she does the same. I take her hand again because it feels good in mine. "Follow me."

We head upstairs to my room. "Wow," she mutters, taking in the super-sized bed in the centre of the room. "You have steps leading up to your bed," she points out, and I laugh. "And those pillows look like the softest pillows in the world."

I point to the walk-in shower at the other side of the room. I could have shown her to one of the private showers in the other bedrooms, but this one is impressive with grey tiles surrounded by glass and a rainfall shower head. When I designed it, I thought about how fucking hot it would be to lie in bed and watch my future wife shower. Plus, Meli mentioned a shower big enough for two when I asked about her ideal date. The thought of Meli being naked in my room drives me insane. "I'll get you a change of clothes and a towel." I turn to leave, and she makes her way to the shower.

# ARTHUR

I wait five minutes before returning, knocking on the door before entering. She's so lost under the rainfall spray, she doesn't immediately see me. When she opens her eyes, she smiles. "I was waiting for you."

I place the towel on the bed. "Not a great idea, Meli. You're drunk."

"Which makes me braver."

"Which makes you think you're making good decisions, when really they're very bad."

"You just ate me out on the roof of your club . . . don't start something you can't finish." She arches her brow in a challenging manner.

I begin to unbutton my wet shirt. "You're telling me you didn't finish?" I tease, moving towards her. "Cos I'm pretty sure half of London heard you finish, Amelia."

She grins, biting her lower lip as I toss my shirt to the floor. "I'm drunk, so my memory isn't that good." I laugh, unfastening my trousers and kicking them off, followed by my boxer shorts.

I grab a condom from a shelf beside the shower. Meli snatches it, ripping open the foil packet. "Allow me."

She pushes me against the wall of the shower and lowers to her knees. I don't usually allow a woman to take control, but it feels important for her to have it, like she craves it.

# NICOLA JANE

She grips my shaft, and I close my eyes, hissing when she moves her hands back and forth. She sheathes my erection in rubber, and I reach under her arms and lift her to stand. I'm getting impatient, and she giggles when I bend her over, forcing her hands against the wall. Lining myself up, I hold her hips as I ease into her. She feels too good, and I pause, trying to regain control of myself. "Shit," she murmurs under her breath, "don't stop."

"Angel, if I don't take this slow, I'm gonna embarrass myself."

"I need it hard and fast," she whispers, her voice breaking as I ease in some more. "Fuck, Arthur, please . . ."

Her begging makes it hard to resist the urge to fuck her like she needs. She tries to back onto me, pushing off the wall, but I dig my fingers into her hips. "We're doing this my way, Meli."

"Fuck me, damn it," she snaps. And that's her issue—she's so used to being fucked and discarded, it's all she knows.

I turn off the water and then grab a fistful of her hair, pulling her to stand slightly and easing in some more. I press my mouth to her ear and use my free hand to gently tease her nipple. "You're not in control here, Amelia," I growl, and she shivers. "I'm gonna take my time and worship every goddamn inch of your body, and you'll take it, understand?"

# ARTHUR

When she doesn't respond, I tug harder on her hair, and she hisses. "Understand?" I repeat.

"Yes, boss," she whispers, and I groan, gently nipping her shoulder. I pull out, taking her by the hand and leading her to the bed. Grabbing the towel, I wrap her up before sitting her on the edge of the bed.

"Open," I tell her, pulling her legs apart. She slowly does as I ask, keeping her eyes on me the whole time. I smirk, staring at her swollen pussy. I lower to my knees and push her to lie back. "You taste too good." I bury my mouth between her legs for a second time, holding her down until she's writhing beneath me and screaming through another orgasm. The second she stills, I spin her onto her stomach. She yelps in surprise when I push into her, placing my legs either side of her and pressing my hands into her upper back. I push to the hilt, and she groans, burying her face into the sheets. I stare down between us, watching as I disappear inside of her. "Say the words," I growl, moving faster.

"What words?" she pants.

"I am perfect."

"No."

I growl, taking her hair again, and lower my mouth to her ear. "Fucking say it," I hiss, slamming harder, "or we ain't finishing shit."

"I am perfect," she cries, grabbing handfuls of the sheets.

"Arthur's perfect angel," I say.

"Arthur's perfect angel," she repeats, shuddering. I feel the warmth of her orgasm on my cock, and I pull from her, removing the condom and coming over her peachy backside. The only sound in the room is our heavy breathing, and I rub the sticky liquid into her skin until the evidence is completely soaked up.

"Now, tell me, Angel, how long do you need before I can do that again?"

# Chapter Nine

MELI

My chest is tight. So tight, I can hardly breathe. *It's happening again.* I feel for my bedside lamp, but it isn't there and I knock something off the side, sending it crashing to the ground. I grip my throat and try to sit up, but I feel dizzy and disorientated. The room is suddenly bathed in light, and Arthur's alarmed expression reminds me of where I am. *Oh god, I did it again.* The realisation only makes this worse.

I gasp harder, each breath becoming tighter than the last. Arthur is speaking, but it sounds muffled as he helps me to sit. I lean my head forward and rest it between my knees. Closing my eyes, I picture blue sea lapping over the sand, tickling my feet and running back out, all the while breathing in and out, in and out. The tightening begins to ease, and I feel the tips of Arthur's fingers tracing circles over my lower back. After a few silent minutes, I relax back against the pillows and stare straight ahead. "Sorry," I mumble.

"Don't be. How long have you suffered from panic attacks?"

"Since I was thirteen."

"There's a bottle of water on the floor. You knocked it off," he says, smiling. "And painkillers on the table. I assume your head is hurting?"

My mouth is so dry, I can hardly speak as I reach for the water and unscrew the cap. "What time is it?"

He grabs his watch from his bedside table. "Seven a.m."

"I should really get home to shower. I have to be at work soon," I mutter, adding a small laugh to hide the fact I'm mortified that I've woken up naked next to my boss. I swallow the pills, and Arthur takes the bottle of water from me, leans across to set it on the nightstand, and catches my jaw, turning my head to face him. He places a kiss to my lips, and I immediately pull back. "I haven't brushed my teeth," I mutter.

"Shower here, with me," he murmurs, grinning and taking his kiss along my collarbone. I briefly

# ARTHUR

close my eyes, enjoying his lips on my skin. He takes my nipple into his mouth, and I shrug him off again.

"I have to go." I try to get out of bed, but he tugs me back to him, hooking his leg over my own and pulling my back to his front. He rests his chin on my shoulder.

"I have a feeling you're pushing me away, Angel," he whispers in my ear, and I shiver. "Just two hours ago, you were sitting on my face and begging me to let you come, and now, you can't even look at me." I feel my cheeks turn crimson with embarrassment. "So, here's how it's gonna work. You'll shower here . . ." He runs his hand over my thigh and down between my legs. I make way for the intrusion, exhaling in appreciation when his fingers brush my swollen clit. "I'll drive you home to change, and then we'll drive to the office together." He pushes a finger into me, and I groan, burying my face into the pillow. I'm already too weak for this man.

---

We shower together, and it's on the tip of my tongue to tell him this needs to stop, but then he drops to his knees and does amazing things with his mouth. When he pulls me down to straddle him, I don't object. I ride him slow, just how he likes it, and although the guilt is eating me up, I push it to one side and take what I want. Just like the selfish bitch I am.

After our shower, he dries me off and hands me one of his hoodies. It's oversized on me, almost coming to my knees. I take a pair of his boxer shorts and slip them on too, rolling them at the top to make them fit better.

He drives me to the club in silence, and when we turn onto the road, I can't hold it in any longer. "Stop," I mutter. "Stop the car." He pulls over, looking concerned.

"Another panic attack?" he asks.

I shake my head. "You can't take me in there," I say, avoiding eye contact. He remains silent. "What we just did, it can't ever happen again." He doesn't reply, and I sneak a look at him through my hair. He's staring straight ahead, gripping the steering wheel. "Rosey likes you, and I've totally screwed her over." He inhales sharply, leans over to my side of the car without looking at me, and opens the door. My heart twists as I unfasten my seat belt.

"I'm sorry," I whisper.

"How long will you punish yourself?" he asks, still looking ahead.

"Rosey's my friend," I say feebly.

"You didn't give a shit about your friend when I was eating you out on the roof of my club. Or when you were riding me in the shower," he snaps.

# ARTHUR

I bite my lip. He's angry. "I'm sorry," I repeat.

He slams his hand against the steering wheel then jumps out of the car and rounds it to where I'm standing. "Don't push me away, Meli. You want this, I know you do. I want this too."

I shake my head, letting tears fill my eyes. "You're my boss."

"I can be more."

I take a deep breath. "I need some time. Can you give me that?"

"It's not a hard decision, Meli. I'm offering you everything. You just have to take the leap." He heads back to the driver's side. "Isn't it time you made yourself happy?" He gets in and drives away.

---

"What time do you call this?" asks Mav as I pass his office. I stop and go in to find Grim with him. They assess my outfit. "You've been out all night?"

"Rosey said you were in your room," adds Grim.

"I'm starving. Have I missed breakfast?" I ask.

"Worked up an appetite, did you?" asks Hadley, coming up behind me and gently tugging a strand of my hair.

I wink. "A lady never tells." I hide the guilt I feel behind a smile.

"I know I said I'd try and back off, but can we please ease me in gently? I'm not ready for this," says Mav. I laugh, heading out his office for the kitchen.

Rosey watches me closely as I lower into the seat next to her. "You lucky bitch," she whisper hisses. "Did you fuck Arthur?" I'm so shocked by her direct question, I stare at her without speaking. "Oh man, I knew I shouldn't have left. I totally should have cockblocked you."

"You're not mad?"

"I'm mad as hell," she hisses. "I wanted him."

"Oh god, Rosey, I'm so sorry . . ." I burst into tears.

Rosey's eyes widen. "Hey, I was kidding. Shit, Meli, relax."

I sniffle, wiping my eyes. "I didn't mean for it to happen." I bury my face into my hands. "Fuck, that's not an excuse."

She tugs my hands away. "Meli, stop crying. I was kidding. You got him first, I missed out, it's no big deal."

"I thought you liked him."

She frowns. "He's a good-looking guy, so I wanted to sleep with him."

"You still can," I sniffle, wiping my eyes on my sleeve.

She laughs. "No offence, Meli, I love you and all that, but I don't want your seconds. I'll find another man to occupy me." She puts a pancake on my plate

# ARTHUR

and kisses me on the cheek. "I have to wake my child up for school. You owe me another night out, one where you don't leave me for Arthur."

I shush her, not wanting Mama B to overhear while she washes up. "It's a deal."

---

I change for work, and Mav drops me at the office. I really hope Arthur hasn't sacked me. I don't want Mav to think I can't hold a job because I messed up again. He follows me up to the office, despite my protests.

Arthur is at his desk, yelling into his phone. He nods at Mav in greeting, and he takes a seat. I set about the papers on my desk. When he ends the call, he slams the phone on the desk. "Bad morning?" asks Mav.

"Something like that," snaps Arthur, glancing in my direction. "I need a plus one for an event this evening. Can I borrow your sister?"

I look up in surprise as Mav shrugs. "If she doesn't mind," he replies.

"I owe Rosey a night out," I mutter feebly.

"Rosey's busy tonight," Arthur says bluntly. "And I'll pay you double time."

# NICOLA JANE

"Haven't you got women for this sort of thing?" Mav asks, laughing. "Meli isn't very mature when it comes to events."

"Mav," I screech, embarrassed.

"I do have women for that sort of thing," Arthur clarifies, "but it's short notice, and Meli works for me now so . . ."

"Settled then," says Mav. "But if I was you, I wouldn't let her drink. She'll either vomit or make a show of herself." He's teasing, but I don't appreciate it and I scowl. His smile falters. "Anyway, what are you doing tomorrow night?"

Arthur stares at me for a second before shaking his head. "Not a lot, why?"

"Poker night at the club. Men only, unless you count the club girls," he says, laughing again.

"Erm, you have an ol' lady," I remind him.

"Clearly, the girls are for Arthur and all the single brothers. Speaking of brothers, bring yours along."

## ARTHUR

Meli's avoiding me. She spent most of the day in the archives, and although it crossed my mind to go up there and show her how good things could be between us, I forced myself to give her the time she's asked for.

Before I leave the office, I place a note on her desk arranging to pick her up for dinner at seven. Then I

# ARTHUR

head to Ma's house. Fridays are always dinner at her house, and not much gets in the way of that.

Albert is standing outside on his phone when I arrive. He disconnects the call and waits for me to get out the car. "I need you to stay calm," he tells me when I join him in the front garden of the small house we all grew up in. We've been asking Ma to move into one of our apartment blocks for years, but she refuses to leave her memories behind.

"When you say shit like that, it makes me lose my calm, Bert. What's going on?"

"She's okay. The ambulance is—"

I push past him before he can finish and rush inside, where Charlie is pacing and Tommy is sitting beside Ma, holding her hand. She's got a bandage wrapped around her head, and when she turns to look at me, rage fills me. Her eyes are black and swollen, and her lip is bloody. "Someone explain," I grit out.

"She was mugged," comes Albert's voice from behind me.

"I'm fine, just a little shaken," Ma reassures us.

"I've called a doctor to come check her over because she's refusing to go to the hospital," says Albert.

"Because I'm fine."

"Ma, you banged your head," says Tommy. "You should get it checked out."

## NICOLA JANE

"Did you see who did it?" I ask.

She shakes her head. "Not really. Three youths. They sounded young, anyway. They had their hoods pulled up and their faces covered."

I glance at Albert. Everyone on this estate knows Ma, and they know we're her sons. No one would have touched her unless they were purposely wanting to gain our attention. "We'll sort it, Ma," I reassure her. "Tonight, you'll need to stay with her," I tell Tommy, who nods.

"I'll stay too," Charlie adds. "We'll get you some fish and chips, Ma, and you can rest."

She smiles gratefully. "You're good boys," she mutters.

---

"She can't stay there," I tell Albert as we head out to our cars.

"You know she won't move, probably more so after this because she's stubborn."

"We need names, Bert, before I begin ripping this estate apart." I don't understand how the fuck someone would hurt Ma. She's like a national treasure round here. But I do know, when I find them, I'm going to fucking tear them apart.

Albert checks his watch. "We have some time, let's pay a few visits."

# ARTHUR

We take my car on a slow drive around the estate we grew up on and now run. It's a poverty-stricken area, but we've put a lot of money into it. "Stop," I say, and Albert pulls in next to the local fish and chip shop. There's a group of youths inside, and it's a good place to start because people talk. As we enter, they quiet down.

The manager nods in greeting. "Mr. Taylor, what can I do for you?" he asks.

"Are these kids giving you trouble?" asks Albert, eyeing the group.

"Fuck you, old man," says one, laughing. "Your time on this estate is done. Didn't anyone tell you?"

Albert's hand reaches out so quick, the youth doesn't have time to react before he's coughing and spluttering and Albert is squeezing his throat. "Is that right?" I ask, moving closer to his face, so he can look me in the eye. "I didn't get that memo, so who told you?"

The other youths scatter, leaving their mate to fend for himself. "You gotta be, what, fifteen?" Albert snarls in disgust. "Who the fuck told you it was okay to speak to your elders like that?"

"There's a war coming," he whispers through gasps. "The E15 boys want this estate."

I laugh. "Go home, kid, and tell your dad I'll pay him a visit to talk about your respect." Albert shoves him hard, and he scrambles from the shop.

"Is he right?" asks the manager, leaning on the counter. "Everyone's talking."

"So, why am I only just hearing about it?" I snap.

He shrugs. "At first, I thought it was bullshit, but as the day's gone on, I've seen them. They're on street corners, dealing and not bothering to hide it."

We've never had problems on our own estate. People just know it's ours. We worked our way up through a gang, took it over, and made it ours. It's how we started out.

We have our own dealers, so we're able to control what's on the streets, and they move our product at a fair price. "I'll call Daryll," says Albert. He's in charge of our runners on the estate who carry the drugs to various points so dealers can sell.

"We haven't seen him for two days," says the manager.

"Fuck, why didn't you call me?" yells Albert. "Why the fuck is everything slipping and I don't know?"

The manager shrugs. "How was I meant to know you weren't in the loop?"

I pull Albert from the shop before he smashes the place up. The second we step out, Albert tries to call our top guy. "I've been trying him since I found Ma," he tells me. "He's not answering."

I check my watch. "I gotta get changed, then pick Meli up."

"You're bringing a plus one?"

# ARTHUR

I nod. "Maybe I should pull out," I mutter.

Albert shakes his head. "No. We want everything to look normal. We carry on. I'll track Daryll and come to the dinner late. Besides, you're better at schmoozing with the big wigs," he says with a smirk. "Drop me back to get my car."

---

Rosey is outside the club when I arrive to collect Meli. "Business or pleasure?" she asks.

"Aren't you supposed to be working?" I ask.

"Just about to go, boss," she says, winking. "Look after her tonight," she adds with a knowing smile.

Inside, I find Meli talking to Rylee. I inhale sharply. She looks stunning in a long red dress and matching heels. It'll go perfectly with my gift. "Sorry I'm late," I say, checking my watch that reads quarter past seven.

"It's fine," says Meli.

"Have a good time," Rylee says as I lead her away.

"Everything okay?" she asks as I open the back door of the car. I slide in beside her, and the driver pulls out of the car park.

"Fine," I say, forcing a smile.

"You're tense," she replies, and I wonder how she knows that just by looking at me. Maybe she's been studying me longer than I realised.

"I got you a gift," I say, ignoring her last remark. I hold out the box, and she takes it cautiously.

"You shouldn't have," she whispers.

"I appreciate you coming with me tonight," I tell her, like it's no big deal. "It's just a small thank you."

She gasps when she opens the box to see the diamond necklace. "Arthur," she murmurs, "it's beautiful."

"It'll go well with the dress," I say, taking it from the box before she can refuse it and unclipping the clasp.

"I can't keep this," she says as I move to put it around her neck.

"It's a gift."

"It looks expensive."

I fasten it in place, taking my time so I can inhale her scent. I gently brush her hair to one side, and she shivers. "Please, Amelia, for one night, just don't battle me on anything."

She turns back to me, frowning. "What's wrong, Arthur?"

I shake my head, running my finger over her leg. I don't want to offload onto her and ruin our night, so I stay quiet. But inside, there's a storm brewing. I can't get Ma's face from my mind, and knowing those little fucking wannabes are out on my streets is putting me on edge. I should have cancelled. I

# ARTHUR

should be out there breaking bones and spreading bullets.

We arrive at the gala a few minutes later, and our driver opens the door. "There's important people here," I tell Meli as we climb the steps to the council house. "Including the chief of police."

"I know him," says Meli. "Through Mav."

"Then you'll know how this goes. We smile, we agree, and we eat."

She smiles, slipping her hand into mine. "Sounds boring."

"It is," I mutter as we enter the large room full of people.

# Chapter Ten

MELI

Arthur seems on edge. He's tense, and the usual flirty banter is completely gone. Instead, he's short in his answers and silent the rest of the time. It's clear this isn't a date and he really did just need a plus one. And I shouldn't feel disappointed by that—I asked him to give me space.

We're seated at a large round table with eight places set, which soon fills up with people I don't know. The last three seats are taken by Jolene Hall and two men. She rushes to sit beside Arthur, leaning over to let him kiss her on each cheek. She doesn't bother looking in my direction, which is fine by me since I've seen far too much of her as it is.

# ARTHUR

"Couldn't your brothers make it?" Arthur asks in a clipped tone. It's obvious he doesn't want her near him, which makes me smile.

"This is Curtis and Danny," she introduces.

"And they are?" asks Arthur.

"Filling in for Leon and Max," she replies. He decides not to push, instead sighing heavily and checking his mobile.

Dinner arrives and the starter is some kind of slime in a shell. I stare at it. "What's this?"

"Oyster," Arthur whispers.

"Didn't we get a choice?"

"Just eat the salad dressing if you don't like it," he mutters, checking his phone for the hundredth time.

"Are you mad with me?" I ask, pushing my plate away.

He eyes the food I'm clearly not going to eat in irritation. "What?"

"You're being really off with me, and I'm trying to work out if it's because you're mad at me for this morning."

"How come you brought the office girl?" asks Jolene, interrupting us.

"That's rude," I mutter, more to myself.

"Excuse me?" she asks, arching a brow.

"Meli, enough," Arthur warns, staring at his phone again. Jolene gives a smirk before tipping the slimy food into her mouth.

"I love oysters," she adds, taking Arthur's and placing it to his lips. He frowns, still staring at the phone but tipping his head back so the oyster slips down his throat. I want to laugh, or maybe scream, because who the fuck does this bitch think she is? He continues to tap away without noticing my discomfort. "You need to look after yourself, Arthur," she says, squeezing his arm in an affectionate manor. "Business can wait while you eat."

"Huh?" he asks, clearly distracted.

"You look stressed," she continues, rubbing her hand over his thigh. He frowns at it before shaking her off. A man from across the table strikes up a conversation with Arthur, and he puts his phone away to talk about planning permission on a new build he wants. The second course comes out and I'm thankful it's steak and salad.

"Rumours are circulating," one of the men at the table says, and Arthur's face hardens. "Is a street gang moving in on your patch?"

"With all due respect," Arthur mutters in a dangerously low voice, "I'm here with my beautiful date, not to discuss street rats."

# ARTHUR

I almost scoff. He's hardly spoken a word to me all evening. Jolene narrows her eyes. "Date?" she repeats. "You're dating your office junior?"

"Junior?" I laugh.

"You've got to be at least ten years younger," she assesses, rolling her eyes.

"Jealousy is an ugly colour on you," I snap.

Arthur glares at me. "Enough," he growls.

I throw my napkin down on the table and scrape my chair back as I stand. "Fuck you," I hiss, grabbing my jacket from the back of my chair and marching off.

The place is busy with people mingling around other people's tables so they can talk business. I look around frantically, trying to find a way out. I spot Arthur rushing after me and curse under my breath. Spotting a fire exit, I head that way and shove the door hard. An alarm immediately sounds and an emergency light flashes above the door. I freeze, not daring to turn around because the entire room is now silent. Arthur presses his mouth close to my ear. "That's not the way out," he whispers.

"No fucking shit," I hiss.

He reaches around me and pulls the door closed. The alarm stops, and I sag with relief. "Now, let's go and sit back down."

The room begins to move again, and voices drown each other out. "No," I say firmly.

# NICOLA JANE

I turn to find him smirking. His hand rests above my head as he stares down at me. "No?" he repeats.

"You've spent the entire evening ignoring me."

He frowns. "I'm confused, Angel. You said you wanted space. And this is a work thing, not a date."

I lower my eyes. "Stop taking her side. She's being rude, and you're letting her."

"When you talk like that, you sound like a teenager," he mutters.

I scowl, then duck under his arm to escape. He pulls me back to him. "Okay, look, at least get through dessert with me. This is a work thing, after all. I'll drive you right home after, but I can't leave early. People are already talking about me."

"Why?" I ask.

"Because they have nothing better to do in their unimportant lives." He takes my hand and leads me back through the crowd without waiting for me to decide. I guess I'm staying for dessert.

Jolene wastes no time in laughing when I sit back in my seat. She gently touches Arthur's arm and leans into him. "That was so embarrassing." Arthur ignores her, and as she continues to stroke his arm, jealousy begins to build. He's paying her no attention, so I should be relieved, but I'm not. I don't want her hands on him, soothing him. "I know a good way to relieve that stress, Arthur," she whispers, straightening his tie.

# ARTHUR

I slam my hand over his, and he looks at me with surprise. "Forget what I said," I hiss, standing. "I don't need space at all." He looks confused, but he stands anyway, and I pull him to follow me. The cloakroom door is the first thing I see, and I cautiously open it, praying there's no alarm.

"Meli, where are we going?"

I pull him inside the room and close the door. "I'm feeling daring," I whisper, taking his tie and tugging him closer. He grins. "And you still look very stressed." I unfasten his belt. "I'm good at relieving stress," I add. He kisses me, and I reach into his trousers, smiling when I find him already hard.

"As great as this could be," he says, stilling my hand, "I'm not having sex with you in a cloakroom."

My confidence falters and I smile awkwardly. Men love spontaneous sex, and I've never been turned down. I decide to go with it since I've already begun, and I lower to my knees, hoping to convince him. "Who said anything about sex?" I purr in my best seductive voice. I try to unbutton his trousers, and again, he stops me. This time, he fastens his belt before placing his hands under my arms and lifting me back onto my feet.

"I respect you more than that," he tells me, cupping my face in his hands. "You deserve to be worshipped, not fucked on some strangers' coats."

"I don't mind," I say, glancing around.

## NICOLA JANE

"I do," he says with a smile. He places a gentle kiss on my forehead then takes me by the hand. "I'll take you home." I force another smile, embarrassment and shame washing over me. I'm mortified.

## ARTHUR

We get in the car and my mobile rings. "Bert," I answer.

"Sorry I didn't make it. I've been dealing with some shit."

"You find out what the fuck is going on?"

"Seems we started a war. The dick we beat up on the Abbey Road estate, he's the brother of one of the E15 elders."

"Fuck," I mutter. It's not what I need right now. I didn't bother to do a full check on the little shitbag because I thought it was a simple job. Or maybe my head was too full of a certain brunette. It's a niggling thought that I immediately push away.

"I've tried to call Leon and Max, but they're not picking up. This is their fucking mess."

"They didn't show to the dinner. Jolene was there with two guys I've never seen before. I think they might be her security, but she didn't go into detail. Look, do we really need this war? We could move Ma out and wash our hands completely."

Albert goes quiet for a minute. "Man, we grew up on that estate. It's ours, and no little rats are taking

# ARTHUR

it. The people there look to us for help, and we can't just wash our hands and walk away. Besides, you think they'll stop there if we don't put up a fight?"

I pinch the bridge of my nose and sigh. "You're right, I know you're right."

"Get your head in the game, Art. You don't have time for women now. This is priority."

I growl in frustration. "You don't need to tell me that," I snap. "Just find me Leon and Max." I disconnect angrily and immediately feel guilty when I see the way Meli is watching me. "Sorry," I mutter. "Work stuff." I was hoping to wine and dine her tonight, impress her with a luxurious gift and a good night. Instead, I've been a complete dick. I guess it's best she finds out now anyway.

The driver stops outside the gates of my house. I forgot to direct him to the clubhouse first, and I can't get out here and leave my driver to drop her home because I don't like the thought of not seeing her home personally. I press my key fob and the gates open. "I'll take you home soon," I tell her as the car rolls to a stop at my front door. "I just have a few things I have to do."

"You really want me out your way tonight," she says.

I groan. "It's not that, Meli. I just—"

"I know, you have a lot on." I nod, knowing she's pissed but unable to soothe her. I don't have the energy right now, and my mind is full of revenge plots. I get out the car, leaving the driver to help Meli out. I unlock the front door and input the code to deactivate the alarm. "There's wine in the fridge. Help yourself. I just have to make a few phone calls and then I'll take you home."

She heads off to the kitchen, and I go to my office. I dial Leon's number, but it rings out. So does his brother's. I call Jolene. "You need help with those stress levels?" she purrs.

"Where are your brothers?"

"I'm not their keeper."

"It's important, Jolene."

"Why don't you meet me, and I'll tell you."

I sigh. "This isn't a game. I need to speak to one of them now."

"Is this regarding your little rundown estate?" she asks.

"What do you know about it?"

"Just what I heard."

I inhale sharply. "Which is?" I hiss.

"That the E15 boys are moving in." I disconnect the call. I don't have time for her games.

I call Albert and tell him, "I spoke to Jolene. She didn't give me any clue as to where her brothers are."

"The names I'm getting off the street belong to brothers. They go by the surname Palmer." Usually, we know all the gang members around the area, but

# ARTHUR

it doesn't ring any bells. "I thought we were done with all this," he mumbles. The office door opens and Meli stands there in nothing but the red heels and diamond necklace. I suck in a breath, unable to take my eyes off her. She smiles, swirling red wine around her glass.

"Me too, Bert, but we're bigger now, better. We took these kinds of idiots on when we were kids and we won. We'll burn London before we give up what we've worked for."

Meli saunters over, moving to my side of the desk and leaning against it. She places her glass to my lips, and I drink some of the wine. I trace circles over her stomach with my index finger. "Should we bring Mav in on this?" I ask.

Meli sniggers, nuzzling into my neck. "Definitely not," she whispers.

"I don't know. He runs some of that area too, plus, it borders his businesses. Who knows where else they'll try and take. Maybe we should give him the heads-up."

I close my eyes as Meli runs kisses along my jaw, unfastening my shirt buttons. "I'll call a meeting tomorrow."

"Tomorrow? Don't you think it's more urgent?"

Meli rubs my erection and traces her kisses down my chest and across my stomach, once again falling to her knees while she unfastens my belt. "You said yourself, this is just a heads-up. If I call him tonight, he's gonna take it more seriously than he needs to."

She releases my erection from my boxers and wraps her hands around it. "I guess. Rumours are spreading like wildfire, though. What if he hears it from someone else?"

I hiss when Meli sucks me into her mouth, letting my head fall back in pleasure as she pushes me to the back of her throat. "*Fuck*," I whisper.

"It is almost midnight. You're right, tomorrow first thing would be better. I spoke to Tommy. The doctor checked Ma over, and she's all good."

"I know, he texted me earlier," I mutter, glancing down to watch Meli swallow me inch by inch. "She's made of strong stuff."

Albert laughs. "Battleaxe," he jokes.

Meli moves faster, pushing me deeper into her throat each time. "I gotta go, Bert," I croak, gripping a hand in her hair and forcing her to take more. She chokes and her eyes water . . . and it's the sexiest thing I've ever seen.

"Did the date go well?" he asks.

I grin, even though he can't see me. "Better than expected." I disconnect, throwing my phone on the desk and fucking her mouth. When I'm about to come, I pull her away and lift her to stand. Turning her away from me, I bend her over my desk, exposing the wetness between her legs. I run my hand

## ARTHUR

through her folds and spread the juices down her thighs. She fidgets, desperate to feel me there again. My mobile rings out, but before I can get to it, she cancels the call, sliding it out of reach.

"Don't even think about it," she whispers.

I reach into the desk drawer and fumble around until I find a condom. The minute I get it on, I push into her, digging my fingers into her hips to hold her in place. "I don't know what you're doing to me, Angel," I pant.

She pushes back against me, taking me deeper. I lift her leg, pushing it out to the side and resting it on the desk. She groans with pleasure, now lying flat against the desk. I feel her tighten, then her body trembles as an orgasm rips through her. I follow, gripping her shoulders and pushing deep into her, holding her there while I release into the condom. I fall over her, exhaustion hitting me, and rest my forehead against her back. "You okay?"

"Uh-huh," she murmurs.

I stand, grabbing a tissue from a box on my desk and removing the condom. I dispose of it in the bin, and before she can stand, I get another tissue and wipe between her legs. "I need to sleep," I tell her, tugging her against me and wrapping my arms around her waist. I bury my face into her neck, inhaling her scent. "Will you stay?"

# NICOLA JANE

She turns in my arms and wraps herself around me. "Nowhere I'd rather be."

"Sorry I've been distant tonight. I don't know how to function when things go wrong."

She smiles, kissing me lightly on the lips. "I hate it when you're not talking to me."

I feel bad. "Angel, I was never not speaking to you."

"Can we start tonight again?"

I smile, brushing my thumb over her swollen lips. "That'd be good."

We shower together in silence, and when we step out, wrapped in towels, she takes my phone again, this time turning it off. "You need one night away," she says, taking me by the hand. "Let me take care of you."

We lie in bed together naked. She lays against my chest and sleepily strokes her fingers over my skin. "I'm sorry you're having a bad day," she whispers.

"I'm sorry I was a prick tonight. I should have cancelled. I'm not good to be around when I'm stressed."

"You can talk to me," she says.

I run my fingers through her hair. "What changed your mind about taking time to think about us?"

She shrugs. "Mainly jealousy," she says with a laugh. "And because I spoke to Rosey. She was fine about us."

"I knew she would be. She's not into me like that."

# ARTHUR

"How can you tell?"

"I know the difference between when a woman wants a fuck and when she wants more."

Meli props her head on her hand to look at me. "How?"

"It's in the eyes," I say with a smile. "You look at me like there's a future."

"I'm tired of hurting," she admits, a sad glint in her eye.

"I'm not gonna hurt you," I tell her, tucking her hair behind her ear.

"You can't promise that. No one can predict the future."

"I guess not, but I can promise that I'll do everything in my power to make you happy rather than sad. Starting with telling your brother."

She groans and falls onto her back. "Great. He'll ruin it."

"I won't let him, but it's important I tell him out of respect. I've not done this, Meli, not for a long time, but there's something about you that makes me want to tell the world you're mine. I'll handle Mav." I roll onto my side, smirking. "Let's play a game."

"You don't seem the type," she teases, also moving onto her side to face me.

"We each ask a question."

She nods. "Okay. Anything?"

"Anything," I confirm. "I'll start. Where did you learn to suck cock like that?" It's meant as a light-hearted question, but a part of me is curious too. She's fucking good, like she's slipped into a guy's mind and learned the exact moves, or maybe she's had a guy teach her.

Meli looks uncomfortable, giving a nervous smile and a shrug, but I see her mind working double time to come up with the right lie to pacify me. "It's a talent."

"That you mastered by doing it a lot, or that someone taught you?"

She goes to sit up, laughing nervously. "What is this?"

I take her wrist, keeping her in the bed. "Just curious, and now you've reacted like that, I'm intrigued. What aren't you telling me, Meli?"

"I thought this was a game? It feels serious."

"Okay, I'll ask something else."

# Chapter Eleven

MELI

I bite my inner cheek to get a grip on my emotions, which are about to boil over. I could be honest. I could tell him that Ripper made me do it over and over until I cried. That he made me vomit numerous times until I did exactly what he wanted me to. Instead, I stay quiet and wait for the next question, which I know will be just as bad and I'll still be unable to answer honestly.

"How many have you slept with?" He won't like my answer, and I imagine I won't like his. He's got at least ten years on me, and he's not exactly lacking in the looks or size department.

"This is a stupid game," I say.

## NICOLA JANE

"Amelia, play the game," he says, pulling me to lie back down. He leans over and takes my nipple in his mouth. He's not playing fair, and I groan. It shouldn't feel so good when he's already taken care of me less than half an hour before.

"I don't know."

He frowns. "You don't know because you don't want to play the game, or because there's been too many?"

"Do you know how many you've slept with?" He nods. Of course, he does, fucking Perfect Peter. I sigh and reply, "Four."

He nods, satisfied. "That's not bad. Why were you so reluctant to answer?"

"Now, your turn."

"Eleven." I arch my brows. I expected more, I'll be honest. "Twelve, I forgot to add you," he says. "Actually, thirteen because—" I put my hand up to stop him talking. "Can you name them?" he asks, grinning like he thinks this game is fun, clearly oblivious to my discomfort.

"Yes, but I'm not going to."

"Come on, amuse me."

"Why do you want to know?" I snap. "It's weird."

"Grim was one. Anyone else from the club?"

"Arthur, why does it matter?"

He kisses me again, and I'm starting to realise this is a distraction technique. "I think your monsters are

# ARTHUR

in that club, Meli. I need to know who they are," he whispers against my lips.

"My monsters are dead," I snap, pulling the sheet and rolling away from him. "Rosey came back and took care of it."

"Ripper?" he mutters. Arthur helped hide Ripper's body, so he knows Rosey took him out.

"So, now you know." I reach over to the bedside light and turn it off. I'm done talking.

I lie awake, unable to stop the thoughts of Ripper. Arthur tosses and turns for another half-hour before he finally gets out of bed. He takes his mobile phone and leaves without another word. That sends my anxiety to another level, wondering what he's thinking. Does he think I loved Ripper, a man double my age? Even if he was to ask, I wouldn't be able to tell him. Where would I even start? Since the day everyone discovered the truth, I haven't spoken about it. Mav arranged for me to speak to a therapist, but it wasn't helpful. She wanted to pick everything apart and delve into the deepest depths of my hurt and trauma. It was places I didn't want to go. I wasn't ready then, and now, it feels too late, like everyone's forgotten, and bringing it up again will only open their wounds.

I hear Arthur downstairs, talking. When does he switch off? He reminds me of Maverick, with too much responsibility to take a break. I close my eyes, drifting into a restless sleep.

---

*Thirteen. I am officially thirteen. I smile across the flickering flames dancing on my birthday cake to my twin sister. Hadley grins wide. She loves cake. Mama B counts to three, and we both blow out the candles. Everyone claps.*

*Dad hands us each a present. They look exactly the same shape and size, as we often get the same stuff. It's the downfall of being a twin. I'm excited. I hinted a lot for a mobile phone. All my friends have one since starting secondary school, aged eleven, but Mav always said I wasn't old enough, and Dad agreed. We rip open the pretty pink paper together. I stare down at the Game Boy box. A Game Boy, what the actual... "Thanks," says Hadley, looking equally as dumbfounded. She'd probably asked for books.*

*"Yeah, thanks," I add, smiling. We give Dad a kiss on the cheek, as it's expected, then we hug Mama B. "Can I go to my room and set it up?" Dad nods, and I rush off, feeling angry tears stinging my eyes.*

*I throw myself onto my bed. Fuck, I told everyone I was getting a new phone. Justin even wrote down his phone number for me. Everyone wants his number. The bedroom door creaks open and Ripper steps in. He locks the door and makes his way over to my bed. I smile sadly as he takes a seat.*

# ARTHUR

*"I got you a present," he says, handing it to me. He's been really nice the last few months. He gets me, and he gets how suffocated I feel at the club. "But you can't tell anyone, not even Rosey."*

*I unwrap the present and gasp. "A phone," I whisper, running my hand over the box. "Oh my god."*

*"I couldn't let my favourite girl down, could I?" he asks, winking. I throw myself at him, wrapping my arms around his neck and squeezing him extra tight, so he knows how much I appreciate this.*

*"You're the best," I say.*

*"But there are rules." He likes rules. "You keep it hidden, you don't tell anyone, and I have full access."*

*"Full access?"*

*"I've set it up. The password is 'Ripper's girl'. You're not allowed to change it. I gotta make sure you're safe." I nod, willing to agree to anything right now. "And no boys. I don't want you talking to no boys." Justin enters my mind, but I nod again. I'll save his name under Justine. "Now, you know I get you anything you want, right?" I nod. "I've always been good to you. You're my favourite. And I know you're at that age now where you're curious about boys." I feel myself blushing. "And so, I wanna help you out. It's normal when you care about someone to show them the way."*

*"Okay," I mutter, frowning and not knowing where this is going.*

*"Meli, have you ever kissed a boy?" I shake my head. I don't get a chance to date when I'm surrounded by bikers. I even get picked up and dropped off to school. "Do you wonder what it's like?"*

*"I guess." I feel embarrassed. It's not the sort of thing I want to discuss with one of the club brothers.*

*"You want me to show you?" I bite my lower lip, shocked he's even suggesting it. Ripper's nice, and all the women at the club fancy him. I hear them talking about him all the time. But he's way older, like almost my dad's age. "I'm looking out for you. What if a boy tries to kiss you one day and you don't know what to do?" I'm pretty sure that'll never happen seeing as I'm not allowed to be free like other teenagers. "And your dad put me on Meli watch, right?" he adds, laughing. The guys take turns watching over me and Hadley. Ripper rides me around when I have to go places.*

*"But, look, if you don't want to, it's fine. I just didn't want the boys at school laughing at you when you don't know what to do." He stands, but he looks annoyed. I hate I've upset him when he's just spent all this money on me, and he's always so kind, thinking about what I need.*

*"I do," I say quickly, and he pauses. "If you're sure you don't mind."*

*He sighs, sitting back down. "Why would I mind helping my favourite baby girl out?"*

## ARTHUR

# ARTHUR

I need to focus, but all I can think about is Meli. Ripper was a lot older, maybe twenty years older. Anger boils my blood. And Maverick must know because he put the call in to ask me to bury Ripper's body under tonnes of concrete. He's now laid to rest under the footings of a new apartment block. That apartment block used to be the garage run by the MC.

Someone buzzes the gate, and I pick up the intercom. Rosey's face comes into view. "It's three a.m."

"I'm aware of the time, Arthur, I own a watch. It's not why I came."

I release the gate and watch out my office window as she skips up the drive. I shake my head. Who the fuck skips when they're an adult? I meet her at the front door, leaning against the frame so she can't come in. "What are you doing here?"

"I did what you asked. I tracked down Dumb and Dumber. Did you know Jolene was screwing another E15 guy?" I frown, moving to the side so she can come in. She goes through to the kitchen, and I follow. "Red wine?" she asks, picking up the half-drunk bottle. "I didn't know you were a fan."

"I'm not."

"You have a guest?"

"Rosey, stick to the point."

She grins, taking a drink from the bottle. I roll my eyes and grab a glass from the drainer, slamming it beside the bottle. She pours half a glass and announces, "They're dead. I called Albert, he's on his way."

It's another five minutes before Albert walks in. He looks tired, and I wonder when the last time he slept was. Probably months ago, like me. "You keep weird hours," he grumbles, taking Rosey's glass and draining it.

"I can't do my kind of work in the daytime," says Rosey. "I'd get caught."

"With the way you work, I'm surprised that hasn't happened," he retorts.

"Leon and Max are dead," I tell him, and he pauses the glass, resting it on his lips. His eyes dart to Rosey, and she nods, confirming it.

"How, when, where?" he asks.

"Their bodies are currently disintegrating in a barrel of acid."

"Jesus," I mutter, pinching the bridge of my nose. "Does Jolene know?"

Rosey shakes her head. "She's having sex with two men, lucky bitch. Dangerous men, apparently."

"Who?" asks Albert.

"Danny and Curtis Palmer."

"Palmer," Albert repeats. "They're high up in the E15 boys. The ones I told you about," he tells me.

# ARTHUR

"Danny and Curtis, they were at the meal tonight," I say. "She introduced them. Fuck, she had them right under my nose and I didn't even realise."

"You think they have anything to do with it?" asks Albert.

"Probably. She's gonna be devastated."

"She might be in danger," adds Rosey.

"I'll call her first thing and arrange to see her. I should be the one to tell her about her brothers," I say.

"Maybe Mav can offer up some shelter for her," suggests Rosey.

"I'm meeting him at ten, I'll ask," I say.

"I need the bathroom," says Rosey, slipping out of the room.

"I'll meet you at the clubhouse at ten," Albert says before heading out.

"Do we need to worry about these brothers, Bert?"

He looks back over his shoulder. "I hope not, Art. I really hope not." I stare at the door for a few minutes after he's left, wondering what this new information means.

I hear a scream from upstairs and run in the direction of my bedroom, I burst in to find Rosey lying beside Meli, both laughing uncontrollably. "Christ, I thought something was wrong," I snap.

Rosey laughs harder. "You thought I wouldn't find out who you had up here? I had to check you weren't cheating on my best friend." She pats the bed. "Imagine, all of us together," she teases.

I roll my eyes. "I've got work to do." I close the door, leaving them to it.

---

Rosey appears at my office door at nine-thirty. She stretches out. "You have the comfiest bed."

I arch a brow. "Glad you had a good sleep."

She grins. "Sorry, were you wanting to climb back in? Yah know, if you're going to date Meli, you need to get used to having me around."

"Is that right?"

She nods. "We're joined at the hip."

"Apart from that time you walked out of the club for years," I remind her.

Her smile fades. "Yeah, well, that was unavoidable."

I throw my pen down and lean back, staring at her. "Why was that?"

She composes herself. "Just because you pay me, doesn't mean I have to tell you my life story."

"Why did you end Ripper?"

She leans against the door frame, trying to remain unaffected by my questions, but I see how uncomfortable this is making her. "Why don't you ask my President that?"

# ARTHUR

"I intend to, but seeing as you pulled the trigger, I'm asking you first."

She walks over to my desk, placing her hands on it and leaning towards me like she's suddenly gained power. "A word of warning . . . you rake up all that shit, and Meli will run a mile."

"Not if I don't let her."

She gives a small laugh. "No one is untouchable, Arthur. She's my best friend, and if you upset her, I'll end you."

I move fast, grabbing her throat, but she's just as fast, taking my sharp letter opener from the desk and holding it to my eye. I grin. The thrill is addictive, and I see the heat in her eyes. "Do it," she pushes. "So I can tell her what a shitbag you are. She'll leave you in a heartbeat."

"You'd love that, wouldn't you? To get between us. But I promise you something, Red. Her and I, we're it. She's not leaving me, and you're not coming between us. I'm gonna marry that woman."

"Then accept there will be parts you'll never see, parts best left hidden."

"To fester and tear her up inside? She doesn't fucking sleep properly, it haunts her. Until I know what that is, I can't help her."

Rosey laughs again, and it's cold. "You're not her saviour. Stop trying to be the hero and just take her as she is."

## NICOLA JANE

I shove her away, and she falls back into the chair behind her. "I am taking her as she is. Nothing will send me running, but there can't be secrets between us. I wanna know it all."

"So it can haunt you too? What's the point."

"The point is, she can't ever move forward until she faces the monsters. Surely, you know that."

She stands and heads for the door. "Sometimes, they're too big to face. The best thing for her is if you love her as she is."

---

I get to the clubhouse, where Albert is outside waiting for me. "Ready for this?" he asks. I nod, patting him on the back.

We head straight for Mav's office. Rylee climbs from his lap, smiling as she passes us to leave. I want that. I want the wife and the love it brings. "Right, what's this about?" asks Mav.

"It's a heads-up," begins Albert, taking a seat, and I join him.

"The E15 boys are trying to move in on Broughton estate," I say. "It's already happening. Our main man, Daryll, is missing." Mav stares open-mouthed. "And we found out Leon and Max Clifton are both dead."

Mav sits straighter. "Are you shitting me?"

# ARTHUR

"We're not worried," Albert says quickly, trying to calm the situation.

"Not worried? I've only heard a small part of this shitshow and I'm fucking worried." He stands. "I'm calling church."

"Look, Mav, now we know, we can get it under control," I begin.

"Now you know," he repeats, "which means they did all this under your nose, and you didn't know. Is that because you're too busy fucking around with my sister?" he yells.

Albert raises his eyebrows. "He's good," he mutters.

"I was gonna tell you about that today," I explain.

He yells for the men to get into church, and one of the prospects rushes past to knock the brothers up from their rooms. "Don't mention my sister in church. I haven't told Grim," he mutters.

"Why's that a problem?" I snap. "I don't owe him an explanation."

Mav shakes his head. "He's the VP of my club, and he's practically her second brother."

"Seems there's a lot of your brothers fucking their way around your sisters," I growl.

He spins back to face me. "What did you say?"

"Tell me about Ripper," I snap.

# NICOLA JANE

His expression changes and he takes a step back. "We need to get into church," he mutters, leaving the office.

"What the fuck was that?" hisses Albert.

"Nothing," I growl, following Maverick.

The men seat themselves around the table, and Mav slams the gavel to shut them up. "We have a situation." He proceeds to fill them in before turning it over to me.

"We don't know much else. I'm about to meet Jolene Hall to tell her that her brothers are dead, but Rosey also said that Jolene is sleeping with the Palmer brothers."

"Both of them?" asks Tatts, laughing.

"Apparently so. Either way, we can't rule out that the brothers got rid of Leon and Max. They could be using her to get to the businesses, which means once they have what they need, they'll end her too."

"These street rats want to get bigger," says Grim.

I nod. "And if they're determined enough, they'll do it. I was once that rat and look at me now."

"The thing is, we worked too fucking hard to let this go," Albert explains. "We don't expect you to fight a war you have nothing to do with, but we needed to give you the heads-up in case these kids wanna step farther than our side."

"We'll vote on it. Wait outside," orders Mav coldly.

# Chapter Twelve

MELI

*It's the middle of the night when Ripper sneaks into my room. It's been a full week since he went on a job with my dad, so this is the first time I've seen him. I sit up, turning the bedside light on. I've been crying, and he sighs. "Baby girl, you know I can't do anything about it." He sits on the bed and brushes the hair from my eyes. "It's not real, the shit that goes on down there."*

*"I heard Scarlett screaming your name," I snap.*

*"What am I supposed to do? If I come back from a week and don't fuck a whore, your dad will ask questions." He places a kiss on my forehead. "I want nothing more than to tell the world about us, but they wouldn't understand, would they?" I shake my head. "Anyway, look, I've got a*

## NICOLA JANE

*present for you." I take the bag. "I heard you telling Rosey you wanted it."*

*Inside is a scarf from Gap that I've had my eye on for ages. I smile. "Now, does that make up for it?" I nod, unsure if I mean it. He kisses me gently. "And you know, I wouldn't have to go to Scarlett if we just—"*

*"You said when I'm ready," I remind him. I'm thirteen years old. I'm scared to do the things he's shown me on the internet.*

*"I know, and I meant it. This is all at your pace. I just want to help you."*

*I nod. I'm lucky to have him, and he treats me really nice, buying me most things I want. The only thing is, I'm not allowed to tell anyone. He thinks they won't understand, but how can they not? I really want to tell Hadley, and maybe Rosey, but I think she'd be really jealous I've got an older man. "I think I'm ready," I say quietly, even though I'm still not one hundred percent sure.*

*He smiles. "Are you sure? Only if you really want to."*

*I nod. He looks so pleased with me, and I like it when I please him. "Will it hurt?"*

*"Only for a second. It'll feel good the more we do it."*

"Earth to Meli," says Hadley, waving her hand in front of my face. "Where did your mind take you?" She's smiling, though she wouldn't be if she knew.

I inhale and force a smile. "Sorry, I was thinking about work."

"And a certain Mr. Taylor?" she asks, smirking.

# ARTHUR

"About that," I begin, and she sits down next to me. "We sort of got together."

"What does that mean?"

"I think you know what I'm saying, Hads," I reply.

"Right, but was it just sex, or sex and a relationship?"

I shrug. "He wants more, more than just sex," I explain, and she grips my arm excitedly. "But—"

"No," she cries dramatically. "No, no, no, don't say but."

I laugh. "But," I repeat, "he wants to know about my past. I think he's guessed something happened."

She smiles sadly, taking my hand. "Don't you want to tell him?" I shake my head. "Meli, you never talk about it. Maybe telling someone would help."

I roll my eyes. "Hadley, he's not my therapist—"

"Because you don't have one," she cuts in, her tone disapproving.

"I can't start laying everything on him like that. He'll run a mile."

"Or he'll appreciate you being honest, and he'll help you move on."

"I have moved on," I argue.

"Huh," she grunts, arching a brow.

"I have," I repeat.

"You don't see a therapist and you haven't told anyone what happened, not really. All I'm saying is, if you don't want to go into details, at least explain who Ripper was and what he did." How do I explain it when I don't understand myself? It's not like Ripper pinned me down and forced me . . . well, not right away anyway. It happened without me knowing it was happening. How the fuck do I explain that?

Rylee comes over. "Anyone know what's happened with Mav and Arthur?" she asks, joining us on the couch.

I sit straighter. "Why?"

"Mav just came out of church and ordered Arthur into his office. He looked pissed. And I've never seen anyone order Arthur anywhere. It was quite the scene."

Hadley grimaces. "You should get in there."

"Why? Do you know what's happened?" asks Rylee. I head for the office, leaving Hadley to explain.

I don't bother to knock because I hear full-on yelling from inside the office. Mav almost shouts at me to get out until he realises it's me. "More secrets," he says. "Fuck, Meli, I thought we were done with secrets."

I scoff at his words, slamming the door closed. "You wanna talk secrets, Mav?" I snap. "Cos you have a big one that you've happily told Hadley about."

## ARTHUR

"When I said I'd ease up, I didn't mean my business associates," he growls. "First, my brother, and now, Arthur."

His words cut deep, and Arthur takes my hand, squeezing it. "You're out of line, Mav," he murmurs, and I feel him trying to stay calm.

"You don't get to tell me I'm outta line when it comes to *my* family," Mav yells. He brings his attention back to me. "Have you thought about how this ends, Meli? What happens when you get bored and walk away, cos I can't cut ties with him."

"It's not going to end," says Arthur impatiently.

"It always ends where Meli's involved," Mav shouts. "She can't fucking commit." He sounds just like our dad, and I feel myself shutting down.

"I want to go," I tell Arthur, and he begins to lead me away.

"The truth hurts, right," Mav mutters.

I spin back to face him. "Have you ever thought about why I can't commit, Maverick?" I snap. "Have you ever wondered why I stick to one-night stands and men who treat me like shit?" He stares at me. "Because I'm terrified of them finding out the truth. Of them seeing how dirty and used I am," I hiss. "So, yeah, I might fuck this up, but at least I'm trying to get on with my life." I go to leave.

"Wait," he says, more calmly this time. "Just . . . I shouldn't have yelled. Don't leave."

## NICOLA JANE

Arthur looks to me for direction, and I love that he's letting me choose. "We'll give you time to cool off. I'll be at Arthur's if you need me." In truth, I need the time away to sort my head out. I'm suddenly being plagued by thoughts of Ripper, he's even back in my dreams, and having Maverick breathing down my neck isn't helping.

### ARTHUR

I love that she chose to leave with me. She trusts me to take care of her, and as she sniffles into a tissue, curled up on my couch, I place a hot chocolate down on the table. "I've not made that stuff in years," I say, and she smiles gratefully. "If you need to talk?"

"I'm fine. Sorry for all this, drama seems to follow me."

I swoop down, kissing her on the head. "It's not a problem."

Albert comes in. "We should make a move," he tells me. I was hoping I'd get out of meeting Jolene, but he clearly isn't letting me off the hook.

Meli smiles. "I'll be fine," she reassures me.

"Okay. I'll be as quick as I can."

---

"So, you and Meli are serious?" Albert asks the second we get in the car.

# ARTHUR

"It's early days, but I like her a lot."

"Enough to go head-to-head with Maverick," he comments.

"He'll cool off. I was never asking permission. I was merely informing him out of respect. What he chooses to do next is his problem, but I'm not letting her go."

"It's our problem if he cuts ties."

I sigh. "He won't. Let him have his tantrum and it'll be all good. Speak of the devil," I say, taking my ringing mobile from my pocket. "Mav," I answer. Some of his brothers wanted more time to think about the vote on whether they should help intervene with E15.

"Looks like we're going to war with these rats."

"Good man. I've got a meet with some of our captains right after I see Jolene. We'll find out what's going on, and I'll get back to you with an update."

"Okay. How's Meli?" he mutters.

"She's safe."

"That's not what I asked," he snaps.

"With all due respect, Mav, and I do respect you, I'm gonna take care of your sister whether you like it or not, and that means I get to decide what I tell you about her, cos right now, I don't think you have her best interests at heart."

"You don't know her like I do, Arthur. If she changes her mind, are you gonna let her walk away?"

# NICOLA JANE

"No."

"Exactly, so you're wrong when you say I don't have her interests at heart. I'm looking out for both of you. If this goes south, I've gotta protect her from you."

"Then let's hope it's doesn't." I disconnect right as we pull up outside Jolene's.

We go inside the apartment block and the security calls ahead to inform her of our arrival. We head up, and she's already waiting at the door looking confused. "Not one, but two Taylor brothers."

"Are you alone?" Albert asks. She nods and steps aside so we can go in.

She follows. "If this is about Leon and Max, I have no idea where they are. I've called and called, and neither are picking up. We had words, but they never usually ignore—"

"It is about your brothers, Jolene," I cut in. She grips the worktop in the kitchen, almost like she's bracing herself for my words. "They're dead."

She inhales sharply. "No. No, they can't be. I . . . how?"

"How well do you know Curtis and Danny Palmer?" asks Albert.

"Not that well," she mutters, frowning. "Oh god, what the hell am I gonna do without them?" she suddenly cries, breaking down. She throws herself against me, and I wrap my arms around her, giving Albert an eyeroll.

"The thing is, we know they're part of E15," Albert continues. "What if they're to blame?" She stops sniffling to look at him. "We think you should move into The Perished Riders clubhouse until we know for sure you're safe."

"No. I'm safe. I hardly see those two, and they wouldn't hurt me. I get on with everyone in that gang."

"Jo, they could be using you to get to the businesses," I say gently.

"You're wrong," she says, "and I'm not staying with the bikers. I don't know them."

"Then stay with Arthur," Albert suggests. I glare at him, and he winks, smirking. "He'll keep you safe."

"I think the club is a better option," I try, but she's already nodding at Albert.

"Great, get a bag together," he says, and she goes off to do that.

"What the fuck?" I whisper angrily.

"We gotta keep an eye on her, Art. We don't know if they want to take everything from under her, and think about it, if they do, they'll have businesses on our estate and Mav's. We can't risk it."

"Can't she stay with you?"

"Nah, I'm always running around for you. Besides, I'm gonna help out with Ma."

"Meli's gonna lose her mind."

"Maybe this is more important, Art. Business comes first."

"Doesn't mean I can't have both."

"It does if you can't move freely. This thing with Meli, it won't work if she doesn't understand the life you lead, especially if she doesn't trust you. You don't need the drama."

Jolene comes back holding a bag. "I'm ready."

"Excellent. We'll take you there before we head out to our meeting," says Albert.

---

Meli is watching television when we get back. Albert takes Jolene's bag. "I'll take this to your room. Arthur can introduce you to Meli." He walks off, grinning. Arse.

I kiss Meli, but she's already eyeing me in that annoyed way she does sometimes. "Angel, you remember Jolene." They stare at each other with pure hatred. "She's gonna be staying for a couple of nights."

"Is that right?" asks Meli coldly.

"She's had some terrible news tonight," I add in the hope this calms her.

"Maybe I could have a word," she hisses, standing and heading for the kitchen.

# ARTHUR

I smile awkwardly at Jolene. "I'll just be a minute."

I close the kitchen door behind me. "Look, Meli, it's unavoidable. Her brothers have been found dead, and I've got to keep an eye on her."

"Great, throw that at me so I can't complain," she snaps.

I laugh, taking her hand and pulling her closer. "It's just a couple of nights."

"You had sex with her," she mutters.

I nod, placing a kiss on her nose. "And I regret it deeply. If it helps, I don't remember any of it."

"That doesn't help," she mutters sulkily.

"I'll explain everything when I get back," I say, kissing her.

She pulls back. "Where are you going?"

"I have a meeting."

"You're not leaving her here with me," she hisses.

"Angel, come on, it's not that bad."

Her eyes widen. "Would you want to sit and drink wine with a man I'd slept with, a man you'd caught me naked with?"

I gently rub my thumb over her jugular. "It wouldn't happen, Angel, because he'd already be dead." I kiss her again, harder this time, stealing her breath. "Now, don't put dark thoughts in my head right before I'm about to leave. Things could turn ugly out there."

# NICOLA JANE

Five of our captains are waiting for us in a secluded, disused factory. Albert shakes hands with one of them. "Mr. Taylor, we've been trying to get hold of Daryll all day. No one's seen him."

"When's the next supply meant to be collected?" I ask.

"It was today," Albert replies.

I frown. "So, no drugs went out at all?" I snap, and Albert shakes his head. "Fuck, we can't have that shit just sitting around waiting for a raid."

"Some of our runners have gone over to E15," one of the men says. "They couldn't miss a day and lose out on money."

"Fuck," mutters Albert. "I'll get the supply out tonight. Have you got enough runners to take it to the selling points?"

They nod. Daryll sorts out the supply house, cutting the drugs and handing it to the runners, who then distribute it to drug houses we have set up. The users collect from there. We have sellers in all our bars and Mav's. That means nothing's selling on our patch tonight, leaving E15 open to fill our users with their shit.

"You got any names for us?" I ask.

# ARTHUR

"Just what we told Albert earlier, boss. The two brothers work under the leaders, but we don't have names above them."

Albert is already on his phone, sorting out the supplies. "Okay. Get word out the flow is back up and running. Any more problems, you call Albert direct." I hand him Albert's business card. He saves the number in his phone, and I take the card back. It's risky tying Albert's number to him, but we don't have a choice.

By the time I get home, it's late and the house is in darkness. I go up to my room, ready to explain things to Meli, and find the bed empty. There's a note on the sheets, and I snatch it up. *Decided to go home. Let me know when your guest has left.* I'm tired, and this is the last thing I need. I try to call, but she doesn't answer, and there's no way I'll get into the clubhouse at this hour. I screw the note up and throw it across the room.

# Chapter Thirteen

MELI

I'm confused. I slowly push myself to sit up, realising I'm on the ground. My head pounds as I look around at the contents of my bag spilled out around me. I remember walking home from Arthur's and trying to call Rosey. *My phone*. I grab my bag, but it's empty and my phone isn't amongst the contents on the ground. *Fuck*. I begin to collect my things, stuffing them in the bag. There's a man walking across the road from me, and he stops. "Are you okay, love?" he asks. I nod, wincing as I push to stand. My ribs hurt. "You're pretty beat up," he says, crossing the street towards me. "Fuck, what happened?"

# ARTHUR

I gently bring my fingers to my face and feel wetness under my eye. He's right, there's swelling and blood. "I think I got mugged."

"Is there anyone I can call, the police maybe?"

I shake my head. "No, it's fine. I don't know my brother's number, and they took my phone."

"Can I at least walk you home?" I nod, smiling gratefully when he holds out his elbow for me to take. "I'm Harry, by the way."

"Meli," I mutter.

"You might need the hospital," he says.

"We have a doctor at home," I reply.

"It's getting ridiculous around these parts lately, and it's not safe to be walking home alone," he tells me.

I nod. "I'm only around the corner. I thought I'd be okay. I was trying to call my friend to meet me, but I think that's when they struck." I stop outside the club. "Thanks," I tell Harry. "I'm good from here."

Grim is on his phone when I walk into the clubhouse. He stares open-mouthed before disconnecting and yelling for Mav to come quickly. Maverick rushes from his office. "Jesus Christ, what the hell happened?"

"I got mugged. They took my phone." I drop my bag and burst into tears, shock finally hitting me. "I was trying to call Rosey," I mumble through my tears. Mav hugs me and tells Grim to find Mama

B. "And they came from behind. I don't remember much, but I think my ribs are broken."

He steps back, assessing me. I lift my top to reveal bruises on my ribs. "Where the hell was Arthur?" he demands to know.

"Working. I decided to come home."

"If he upset you and made you leave," he begins.

"He didn't. He doesn't know I've left."

Mama B gasps when she sets eyes on me. She takes me to the kitchen and helps clean my face. She gives me a mirror, and I cry harder. I have a cut under my eye where I've been punched and both eyes are swollen and bruised. My lip is busted, and my ribs are in unbearable pain.

Hadley rushes in. "Grim just told me," she cries, taking my hands. "Are you okay?"

"I think so, a little shocked."

"Should I call Arthur?" she asks.

I shake my head. "He's got a lot on right now. I'll speak to him tomorrow." I don't want to pull him away from whatever it is he's dealing with, and he'll be upset I walked out because of Jolene. After he left, things became awkward, especially when she talked about how supportive Arthur was being. I got jealous and let her get the better of me. It was stupid of me, looking back now.

Hadley helps me upstairs and waits while I change into something more comfortable. "I think Arthur would want to know," she says as I carefully get into bed and take the painkillers she offers me.

"He's got Jolene staying at his place," I tell her. She lowers to sit on the bed. "Before we were a thing, he slept with her."

"That's why you walked home alone?" I nod. "Meli, you could have called me."

"I was trying to call Rosey, but then this happened. Am I being unreasonable?"

"You're insecure, he'll get that."

"Will he?" I ask, shaking my head. "I should have stayed and talked to him."

"Hindsight is a great thing," she says, smiling. "Get some rest. I'll keep checking in on you."

*I pace my bedroom waiting. He usually comes in late. I check my watch just as the door opens and Ripper steps inside. He smiles, closing the door and grabbing me, pulling me against him and burying his face in my neck. "I missed you, baby girl."*

*"I want to talk," I announce, and he pulls back to look at me with an amused expression.*

*"You do?" I nod. "Okay, but before that, can I give you my gift?" My stomach aches. I hate his gifts because I know what they mean. More secrets. More things he wants to do that I'm not ready for. He pulls a small box from his pocket*

*and opens it. It's a charm for my bracelet, the one he got me last week for my fourteenth birthday.*

*"Thank you." I take it and close the box. I've learned over time that he doesn't like it when I try to refuse his gifts. I take a deep breath before announcing, "I think we should stop doing this." This isn't the first time I've mentioned it, but each time, he talks me around and, somehow, I agree to carrying it on, even though I don't want to.*

*"Doing what, baby girl?" he asks, smiling in that condescending way he often does.*

*"This," I say again, pointing back and forth between us. "I don't want you to come to my room anymore."*

*He grins. "Is that so?"*

*I nod. "Lucy said a boy her age taught her to kiss."*

*"Perfect little Lucy," he mutters. He hates all my friends.*

*"And nobody laughed at her because she got it wrong a couple of times. I don't think boys will laugh at me, Ripper."*

*"Of course, they won't, because I taught you what to do. I showed you everything you know, and now, you wanna just leave me? It don't work like that." He moves closer, standing over me. "You don't get to decide when I end this."*

*My heart is beating out of my chest, and my palms are sweating. "Then I'll tell someone," I almost whisper.*

*He laughs, putting his ear closer to my mouth. "Say that again, Amelia."*

*"I'll tell my dad."*

*He grabs my throat and lifts me to stand. "What will you tell him exactly?" he growls. "How you asked me to teach you how to fuck a guy?" He spits the words angrily. "Or how you've been happily taking my gifts, you ungrateful little bitch?"*

*"I didn't want to," I cry out, and he slams a hand over my mouth.*

*"You're a cock tease, Meli, and everyone knows it. Your dad, your brothers, all the guys here think it. You walk around the place dressed like a hooker and expect men not to think you want all this? They'll never believe you over me. I'll tell them how fucking obsessed you are with me." He squeezes my neck harder. "I've given you a fucking year," he hisses, "and you'll leave me when I say you can." He shoves me onto the bed, grabbing a fistful of hair while he unfastens his belt. "And if you tell anyone, I'll go to Hadley instead, and when I've taught her how to be a good little cocksucker like you, I'll slit her fucking throat."*

## ARTHUR

I call Meli again. She's still not taking my calls. "Coffee?" asks Jolene, grabbing the pot and topping up her cup. I shake my head and open my laptop. "Do you always work?" she asks, taking a seat at the kitchen table. She's wearing a shirt that just about covers her arse.

"Have you decided what you're doing about your brothers?" I ask.

"I'm going to report them missing, Albert said it's best to, so it doesn't look suspicious."

"Do you need help with the businesses? I don't know how involved you are in that side of things."

"I'm fine. I know what I'm doing. Maybe I could borrow your little assistant sometime to help in the office," she suggests, laughing.

"Meli is my girlfriend, one day to be my wife, so show some respect."

She's not put off. Instead, she pulls her knee up to her chest, not caring that her shirt's ridden up to reveal her underwear. "Really? She doesn't look like your type."

"And what is my type?" I ask, feeling irritated.

"Someone strong," she begins.

"Meli is the strongest woman I know."

"Loyal."

"You don't even know her."

"And able to handle you."

I smirk. "She can handle me." I slam the laptop closed. "I thought you'd be more upset over your brothers," I say, collecting my things.

"I don't think it's hit me yet," she mutters.

I leave, shaking my head. Something feels off, I just can't put my finger on it.

# ARTHUR

I meet Albert at the office. He looks as exhausted as me. "You seen Meli?" I ask, unlocking the office door and noting she isn't here yet.

"No, didn't she stay at yours last night?"

I shake my head. "No. I don't think she was too happy with my guest, thanks to you."

He grins, taking a seat. "In other news, rumour has it that a woman was attacked last night. The streets are getting bad, Art. It looks like we're losing control to everyone looking in."

I growl and mutter, "And there will be a lot of people looking in."

"I've got the soldiers out there and recruited a hell of a lot more. We got cousins and brothers of kids already running for us. But there's gonna be some losses. That's gonna look bad on us."

"Then let's get out there."

"Not a good idea," he says. "We've come a long way and we have a lot to lose if we get caught hurting any of these guys. Will Meli visit you in prison?"

"We've got to start rattling some cages, Bert. Ma was hurt on our streets, and I can't let that go. We've got to pay some visits in person, get more names, so we can take them out one by one until we get to the top." My patience is gone. I want this done with, and I want the fuckers who hurt Ma.

"What about the Palmer brothers? Get Jolene to lure them for a meeting. We can turn up."

## NICOLA JANE

I nod, getting on my phone.

---

Mav is acting shady when I turn up to the club. He rushes to get me into his office and gives Rylee a look which tells me she's also hiding something. "I came by to give you an update," I say, taking a seat. "I'm waiting for Jolene to arrange a meeting with the Palmer brothers so we can ambush, although I have to be honest, she's acting odd considering her brothers are dead."

"In what way?" he asks, his eyes darting to the window looking out over the club.

"She's not upset, or even quiet. Maybe it hasn't sunk in yet. Anyway, I've got guys out on the streets in force today. We're getting things under control."

"I had the chief of police on the phone this morning. He was telling me the crime rate's through the roof this week. Two stabbings came in while we were on the phone."

"He called to tell you that?"

"No, it was about something else. So, do you need me to do anything?"

I shake my head. "No. I just wanted to update you." I stand. "Is Meli around?"

"No. Something about shopping," he mutters, waving his hand dismissively.

# ARTHUR

"She didn't show for work."

"Oh. Maybe Rylee mentioned she was sick, I can't remember. You know what women are like. Shall I get her to call you?"

"You're acting weird. Yesterday, you were mad as hell, and now, you're . . . not mad."

"Meli's right, it's her life. Did you guys fall out?" The door opens, banging back against the wall, and Grim fills it, looking angry as hell. "Grim, leave it," warns Mav.

"She's a fucking mess," he snarls. "A few weeks and she's already embroiled in whatever is going on in your fucked-up life," he growls.

"What are you talking about?"

"Christ, Grim, she didn't want him to know yet," Mav snaps, then he stands and rounds his desk. "She was jumped walking home from yours. It was a street robbery is all, but Grim's got it in his head it's to do with everything that's happening right now."

I don't wait to hear the rest. I head for her bedroom, bursting in to find her sleeping soundly. She doesn't stir, so I quietly close the door and move closer. I inhale sharply, shocked at the sight of her. Her face is bruised and her eyes are swollen. My hands ball into fists, and I want to hurt the fucker that dared to touch her. I take a snapshot and send it to Albert.

***Albert: Fuck, what happened?***

## NICOLA JANE

*Me: I think she's the woman you told me about earlier, the one that was attacked.*

*Albert: I'll start asking questions. We'll find whoever did it.*

*Me: Two people have to die today, Bert. Today. One for Ma and now one for Meli.*

I kick off my shoes and slip out of my jacket, then crawl into bed behind her, wrapping my arms around her and burying my face into her hair. She stirs, stretching before groaning in pain. I sit slightly, lifting her T-shirt to see more bruising. "I'm gonna fucking kill whoever did this," I whisper.

Her eyes open. "What are you doing here?"

"I thought you were mad at me, so I left you to cool off. If I'd have known, I would have—"

She removes my hand. "I haven't told my brother because he would lose his mind," she says, wincing as she pushes to sit up. "But my memory came back to me, and the men who did this wanted to send you a message." My blood runs cold. "How did they know about us, Arthur? We've only just started seeing each other."

"I don't know," I mutter, confused. For once, I'm lost for words.

"I was two streets away from home. And they weren't following me—they just turned up like they knew I'd be there."

"What did they say?"

# ARTHUR

"That you should take the warning and step away before things get ugly. They took my phone, so they have all my contacts, including you. They told me they would rape me next time."

"That won't happen," I snap, getting up from the bed. "I'll fucking kill whoever did this."

"You don't even know who they are," she screams. "They could have killed me."

I rub my forehead, trying to work out a plan. "Why were you out alone, Meli?" I snap, then instantly regret it. "That's not what I—" I begin.

"Fuck you, Arthur. I should be able to walk home at nine o'clock at night without worrying your crazy enemies will get to me. And if you hadn't brought Jolene home, I wouldn't have left."

"I told you I'd explain that it was unavoidable," I argue. "And if you'd have told me you wanted to leave, I would have taken you myself."

She scoffs. "In between emailing, answering calls, and rushing to your next meeting?"

"That's my life, Meli. I can't put it on hold for you."

She takes a breath. "You're right, so don't."

I pinch the bridge of my nose. "We're not talking about that again. Walking away isn't an option."

"It's not up to you," she snaps.

"It is, Meli. It is up to me!" I yell angrily. She sinks back, putting more distance between us. "It's not an option," I repeat more calmly.

We fall silent for a moment and then my phone rings. She arches a brow, and I sigh heavily, placing it to my ear. "Bert," I say, stepping from the room.

"It was two men. Our guys have them."

"Quick work," I mutter. "Where am I headed?"

He reels off an address, and I disconnect and go back to Meli, who's staring straight ahead. I put my shoes on, then my jacket. "The last man who said those words to me was Ripper," she almost whispers. I still, letting her words sink in. "He spent years abusing me." She confirms exactly what I thought. "And he refused to let me walk away for most of my teenage years. He told me it wasn't up to me either."

"I'm not like him," I growl angrily.

"So, let me walk away."

I shake my head, leaning down to kiss her on the cheek. "I can't," I whisper. "It's not that easy. I'm coming back here after I've dealt with this, so we can talk it through. I want it all, Amelia, the whole truth, and then we'll work through us."

"You're not listening, Arthur. I don't want you to come back."

"You do," I say firmly. "You're pushing me away and this was the perfect excuse. But I'm not letting you ruin this. The men who dared to fucking touch what's mine will pay, and nothing will ever happen to you again. I promise." I press my lips to hers, and she lets me. "I'm gonna go to war for you, Angel."

# ARTHUR

The warehouse is miles out from anywhere, and as I turn off the dark road through the gates, I decide it's the perfect place to take people who piss me off. I'll ask Albert to check if it's for sale, since I have a feeling we'll need a space like this over the next few weeks.

I step inside the warehouse, and Albert is reading a newspaper. Rosey is on her mobile, and two men are tied to chairs. "Busy?" I ask, and they all look my way.

Rosey tucks her phone away. "I was passing."

"Passing here?" I ask doubtfully.

"Passing Albert, and I offered to help."

Albert closes the newspaper. "I didn't want to start without you," he tells me, ignoring Rosey's odd explanation. He rolls open his array of tools. "Who are we starting with?"

I go around to the back of the chairs to check which one is wearing rings. I pat the biggest of the two on the head. "This one."

"Good choice," says Rosey. "He was the rudest when he realised I wasn't going to blow him off."

I remove his gag. "You know me, right? Seeing as you left a lovely imprint of your ring on my woman's cheek along with your message."

"I was just the delivery guy," he spits.

"From?"

"I don't know."

I punch him, and his nose splits, spraying us both in blood. "Try again."

"I don't fucking know, man, alright?" he yells.

The guy next to him is making noises like he's got something to say, so I remove his gag. "The Palmer brothers hired us, but that's not who the message was from," he says in a rush.

"Keep talking," says Albert, removing his favourite knife from its leather pouch.

"Man, shut the hell up," says his friend. "They're not gonna kill us for beating some bitch up."

I hit him again, and he spits a tooth out on the ground. "You're underestimating how much I like her," I warn. "How did you know where she was?"

"A tip-off," says the talkative of the two. "We were told where she was heading."

"By who?" asks Rosey, taking another of Albert's knives and examining it.

"You really are a dumb bitch," yells his friend. "We already told you, we don't know."

Rosey sits on his lap. "I don't like your tone," she tells him. "I like a man with manners."

"Like I give a fuck," he snaps.

She stabs the knife into his thigh, twisting it. He growls, throwing his head back. Rosey jumps up be-

## ARTHUR

fore he can bring it forward to headbutt her. "Now, now, let's not get upset. You totally deserved that."

"Jesus fucking Christ," he grits out, and I roll my eyes. If he can't take that sort of pain, he'll surely squeal like a canary when we start removing skin.

"Not even he can help you," says Albert.

"We really don't know who's at the top," says the other guy.

I remove my jacket and lay it neatly to one side. "I need you to take a message back to the mystery man at the top," I say, rolling up my sleeves. "These are my streets, and I'm not giving them up for anyone." I lay into them, releasing every bit of frustration that's been building since Ma got hurt. When I'm out of breath and covered in blood, I step back. "Remove his fingers," I tell Albert, pointing to the guy with the rings.

Rosey slaps him hard to wake him. "Wakey wakey," she sing-songs. "You haven't heard the whole message yet." He groans. I wipe my hands on a rag, closing my eyes and enjoying the sound of him screaming as he loses each finger. "You miss this," says Rosey gleefully.

"Meli told me about Ripper," I say, and her eyes widen in surprise.

"Good."

"That's it?"

"Yeah, she trusts you. That's good."

# NICOLA JANE

"Maybe," I mutter, pulling my sleeves down. "Help Albert with this and the clean-up. Don't let them go until they're close to giving up, I want them to get a glimpse of Hades."

# Chapter Fourteen

MELI

Arthur walks into my bedroom with confidence just two hours after he left. He drops a bag on the floor by my drawers. "I need space for my clothes," he says.

I take a drink from the glass of water Mama B just left me. "What for?"

"Because I'm staying."

I laugh, but when he doesn't join me and I realise he's serious, my smile fades. "You can't stay here."

"I'm staying, Meli. Mav's fine with it."

"I'm not," I snap. "Besides, you have a guest to take care of."

"I'll check in with her, but I'm staying in this room every night, with you."

# NICOLA JANE

"Until when exactly?" I ask. "It's not practical. My room isn't made for two. It's also ridiculous seeing as you have a huge house, and how long before you're taking another important call and rushing off? Just do us both a favour and go."

He takes off his shoes, followed by his jacket. "Ripper," he says, hanging the jacket on the chair in the corner, "is lucky he's dead." I don't want to talk about Ripper, so I pick up my new mobile phone that Mav got me, and pretend to be engrossed in it. "And if I could kill him all over again, I would. I'd do it slow." He sighs. "Meli, I'm not gonna walk away. Know that every time I go out that door to sort business, I'm coming back to you. I'm gonna protect you from now on. No more monsters."

I lean back against the headboard. "What if you die?"

"I won't."

"Someone might kill you."

He grins. "They might. That's not technically my fault, so you can't be mad at me for that."

"I can. Don't tell me you're not leaving if there's a chance you might die," I say, shrugging.

He laughs. "Okay, I'll try not to die or get killed, but there is a small possibility, like there is with everyone, that it could happen. And if it does, I want you to know I'm truly sorry and I never meant to leave you."

# ARTHUR

I put my mobile down. "All jokes aside, Arthur, this could be a train wreck."

"I'm quite good at staying on track," he whispers, making his way to the bed. "I'm sorry you got hurt. It should never have happened. I've dealt with it, and from now on, I'll make sure you're safe all the time."

"Are they dead?"

He shakes his head. "I need them to relay a message back. They haven't made it in one piece, though."

I nod, glad. They deserve it. "Did you find out how they knew?"

He shakes his head. "No, but there's a strong possibility someone's watching the house."

"Isn't Jolene there?"

"Rosey and Albert are taking it in turns watching over her."

I feel a pang of jealousy that he's watching out for Jolene. It's ridiculous, he's being a nice guy, but it bothers me. She's got her sights set on him, and the fact he's helping her makes her think she's in with a chance. Maybe she is . . . I frown, wondering if I could really let him walk away if he chose her over me.

He lays between my legs, propping his chin on his hands to look at me. His blue eyes twinkle as he grins, showing off those bad boy dimples. "Do you forgive me for everything?"

"Yes." I lean down to kiss him and hiss when my ribs ache. He lifts my shirt and kisses the dark bruising there instead. "Because you don't listen to me when I tell you to go anyway."

"Will you tell me about Ripper?" he asks, bringing his eyes to me again. "I know it won't be easy to hear, but it'll make the awful scenarios in my head go."

I bite my lower lip. "It's not as bad as everyone makes out," I whisper, gently running my fingers through his hair. He closes his eyes. "I know it was all wrong. I see that now, but back then, when I was just a kid, I thought he loved me, like a boyfriend loved a girlfriend." His eyes open again, and he looks sad. "And I can't tell anyone that because . . . because they'll think I wanted him to do that stuff, and I didn't. I just didn't know it was wrong." Tears balance on my lower lash. "Does that make sense?"

He nods, taking one hand and linking our fingers together. "It makes perfect sense."

"I thought he was being nice. It started with a mobile phone." I release a shuddery breath. "If I'd have known what it would mean to take that phone, I would never ever have taken it. But he made it seem so normal, like it was a nice thing he was doing. I spoke to a therapist when it all came out, and she said it's how a lot of men like him start—a gift that tells them if you're going to keep secrets from your loved ones. And I did," I wipe my eyes, "I kept it a

# ARTHUR

secret because I wanted a phone so badly, and when I think about it now, it seems such a stupid thing to be desperate for. Why did I even want a phone at that age? Who was I going to call?" I laugh, but it's empty.

"Peer pressure is a big thing when you're a teenager."

I give him a watery smile. "I was in the popular group, and the pressure to be amazing all the time was full-on. When he offered to show me how to kiss, I said yes. There was a boy at school I liked, and I was nervous because I hadn't kissed anyone before. Mav and Grim made sure of that." He laughs, kissing my hand that's still entwined in his. "It was just a kiss," I whisper, "but he did it a few times, and when I didn't want to, he'd look upset, and I hated that too. He'd been nice, buying me things, and I felt like I was being ungrateful if I said no. So, I let him kiss me a lot. And, of course, that soon got boring because he was an adult and adults do adult stuff." I wipe my eyes again.

"That's what he said, adults do adult stuff, and I remember thinking, *but I'm not an adult yet*. But he started slow, yah know, so I almost made excuses in my own mind. Weeks in and he was telling me he liked me, that I was his. He made me think I should be flattered because he was Ripper, all the women at the club wanted him, and he'd chosen me. He said it was an honour when a biker chose his ol' lady."

"Didn't Maverick or Grim know anything? They watched you so closely that you couldn't even get a first kiss with a boy you liked."

"They watched me outside the club, but inside, we were all safe. Besides, Dad put Ripper on me as my minder. He came most places with me, and it wasn't unusual to see us together a lot."

"He kind of laid claim to you?"

I nod. "But in secret. He said the club girls would turn on me, probably beat the crap out of me. He said his brothers and my dad wouldn't understand what we felt for one another. One time, he came back from a long run with the others. I heard him having sex with a club girl, and I cried. He caught me, thinking I was jealous." I take a breath. "I wasn't. I was relieved. I thought maybe he'd changed his mind and I'd finally be free." I shake my head. "But I wasn't. That was the first night he raped me. We'd spent so long doing other stuff, I didn't think it could get any worse. I was wrong." I can see the pain in Arthur's eyes, and I cup his face. "I'm glad he's dead. I wish he'd suffered more."

"I can't believe no one saw anything," he mutters angrily.

"My dad did." Arthur looks up at me in surprise. "But he blamed me. He said I dressed like a whore,

# ARTHUR

so how could he blame his Vice President for treating me like one. I reminded him of my mother, and he hated her because she had an affair with Crow's dad. But after that, Ripper wasn't left alone with me again, and Dad put a lock on my bedroom door. He must have had words with Ripper because he never knocked again. That was when I was sixteen."

"He abused you for three years?"

I nod. "Of course, then Dad died, and Ripper tried to bully me into having sex with him. By then, I think I'd become an obsession." I frown, unsure. "Or maybe he hated how confident I was. He enjoyed seeing me scared."

"Did you . . ."

I shake my head. "No. He was cruel and aggressive to me whenever people weren't looking, but there was no way he was going to ever lay a hand on me like that again."

## ARTHUR

I lie beside Meli, with her wrapped in my arms, and I stare at the ceiling with her words circulating in my head. How can someone fucking hurt a kid? She was a cute thing, I've seen the pictures on her mirror of when she was younger, and she looked so innocent. He took that, and it makes me sick to my stomach.

"If you keep thinking about it, it'll drive you mad," she whispers into the darkness.

I kiss her on the head. "Sorry. I'm just processing."

"What helps to calm the beast inside?" she asks, running her hand down my stomach.

I catch it before she can touch me. Sex is the last thing I want right now. "Usually, I kill someone."

She scoffs. "Can I nominate Jolene?"

I laugh. "Or I go to the gym."

She groans. "It's midnight."

"I think you're pretty fucking amazing," I say, drawing circles on her back with my fingers. "I'm happy you told me."

"Me too," she murmurs. "Maybe I'll sleep better tonight."

"I'm here to chase the bad dreams away, Angel."

---

I wake early, leaving Meli to sleep. She tossed and turned for most of the five hours I laid with her. I didn't sleep a wink, not because she was unsettled, but because I need to spill blood. It's too late to make Ripper pay, but I can take the anger I feel and turn it on the E15 crew.

I bang on Albert's door, and he yanks it open in anger. "What the fuck?" Then he realises it's me and frowns. "Is Ma okay?"

# ARTHUR

"Yeah, it's nothing to do with that," I mutter, pushing my way inside and going through to the kitchen. "Did you talk to Jolene last night?"

"Yeah, she insists she doesn't have a way to contact the Palmers. She said the three of them had a weekend of fun, they escorted her to the function you were at, and she's not seen them since. They didn't ask anything about her brothers or the businesses. They didn't make her suspicious at all, and as far as she's concerned, it was lots of sex and nothing more."

"It's too much of a coincidence, don't you think?"

"Maybe, but we're no closer to getting our hands on them. Everyone we speak to says they're making lots of noise but they're not showing themselves. It's like they're fucking ghosts."

"Then let's go and make more noise. I want them to come out of the woodwork, and I want to know who the fuck they work for. Get dressed."

He groans. "It's five-thirty."

"Exactly. Let's go hunting, it's been a while."

He goes to get ready, and when he returns, I'm already at the door waiting. "Why are you so keen?"

"The early bird catches the worm and all that."

"No, it's more than that," he says. "You've got a fire in your eyes. I know you, Art, something's bothering you."

## NICOLA JANE

We head out to his car. "Meli was abused as a kid. By one of the MC, Ripper. He groomed her."

"Ain't he dead?"

"Yep, that's the problem. I can't fucking kill him, so I need to hurt someone else."

He grins, unlocking the car. "Gotcha. Well, let's go on a spree."

We begin at one of the bars on E15's streets. The landlord here let's gang members use the bar for meetings as well as selling their gear, so it's their well-known hangout. Albert uses a crowbar to break the lock on the back door, and we go through to the empty bar. The staff haven't tidied up from the previous night, so I sweep my arm along the bar, knocking glasses and bottles to the ground. They smash and I take a seat at the bar, waiting for the landlord. He runs down the stairs a minute later, in his underwear and waving a baseball bat around, but Albert is already waiting for him behind the door, taking the bat from him and shoving him towards me.

"Good morning, Donnie. Sorry about that, I'm a clumsy fucker."

"Jesus, Arthur, what's going on?" he asks, looking around at the broken glass.

"I'm having a bad week, Donnie. A very bad week."

# ARTHUR

He glances nervously at Albert before resting his hands on the bar in front of me, trying to look less nervous. "Okay, how can I help?"

I slap him hard on the shoulder, and he winces. "See, that's the sort of words I need to hear right now. Someone willing to help."

He swallows hard, nodding. "Of course . . . anything."

"Where can I find the Palmer brothers?" He begins to step away, shaking his head, but I reach forward, grabbing him around the back of his neck and dragging him over the bar. I push my face close to his. "Now, now, Donnie, you said anything."

"I can't help yah, Arthur. I don't have a clue where the fuck they are or who they're working for."

"You haven't heard a thing working behind this bar when they're all in here shouting their mouths off?" asks Albert. Donnie shakes his head. "Bullshit."

"I swear it, they don't talk to me about that crap. You know I hate being on this estate. If I could sell up, I would."

"I'm not here to listen to your pity party for one," I hiss, slamming his head onto the bar top. He tries to fight me off so he can get away, but Albert goes behind him, pulling his hands behind his back and zip-tying them together. "I want fucking answers." He looks up, his nose bleeding and maybe his teeth.

"Yah hear about my ma being robbed?" I ask, and he nods. "And then my missus?"

"Fuck, I didn't know you had a missus, Art, sorry to hear that," he mutters.

"No one knows about her, Donnie, which is why I find it fucking odd they knew exactly who she was and where she'd be."

"Okay, look," he takes a breath, "someone new is running the show. I don't know who it is, they're keeping quiet. I don't think half the runners know who it is."

"But the Palmer's will know?"

He nods. "More than likely. They take the orders and hand them down to the runners. They must know."

"What happened to whoever was in charge before?" asks Albert.

"Rumours went out that he was killed a few weeks ago. He was getting too old for the drugs game, the kids were restless, all trying to take over themselves. There was a lot of inner wars going on, and now the streets are a warzone," he says sadly.

"You get the word out there that I'm taking them back," I say, straightening his shirt and patting his shoulder. "I want E15. Tell the restless kids to contact me, I'll make them a good deal." I slide my card across the bar. "And you let everyone know, the

# ARTHUR

Palmer brothers are wanted and I'll pay a lot of cash to whoever gives them up."

I head for the door, Albert following. "What about this?" asks Donnie, turning to show his hands still tied. "And how much?"

We leave without answering him. Those who enquire about a price will be on my list of visits. Some fucker knows where the Palmer brothers are, and it won't take long for them to come running.

# Chapter Fifteen

MELI

I wake to find Arthur gone. I decide to head into work. My ribs still hurt, so I'll stick to light duties, but it'll do me good to get out of here. Mav offers to drive me in his car, seeing as a bike would be too painful. He also tells me to call him when I'm done because I'm not to go anywhere without an escort.

Lola, the bar manager at Artie's, looks relieved to see me. "I tried calling Arthur," she says, "but he didn't pick up. What the hell happened to you?"

"Nothing, don't worry. What's wrong?"

"A woman called Jolene is up in the office. She had a key, so I'm sure it's all fine. I just wanted to check."

I reassure her with a smile and head straight up, wondering what the fuck she's playing at. Jolene is

# ARTHUR

looking at a file when I walk in. She doesn't look alarmed to see me, so maybe Arthur okayed it after all. "Hey, anything I can help you with?" I ask, dumping my bag.

"Nope. I was hoping Arthur would be here. He didn't come home last night." She drops the file on his desk and sits down.

I laugh at her words, rolling my eyes. "You sound like his wife."

"Maybe one day."

I scoff. "Excuse me? You know we're together, right?"

"Please, it makes much more sense for him to marry someone like me, and now I have all my brothers' businesses, it would make us unstoppable. We'd be so powerful together."

I refuse to let doubt cloud my mind and smile confidently. "You shouldn't be in here unless Arthur or I are around. How did you get a key?"

"From home, obviously. I was worried about him, so I came to check he was okay."

"Thanks for your concern, but he's fine. He was with me last night."

She places her elbows on his desk and leans forward. "What happened to you, anyway? I hope Arthur isn't responsible for those bruises. I know how rough he can be when he's horny."

# NICOLA JANE

I force a smile. I'm not in a fit state to bitch-slap her. "I'll tell Arthur you were looking for him. I have a lot to do," I say, opening my laptop in the hope she'll take the hint.

"I can wait."

I send off a text to him telling him to get here now before I start a war of my own with Jolene fucking Hall. It's ten minutes before he walks in the door. "Jolene," he says coldly.

She bursts into tears and rushes to him. I arch a brow and watch the performance. "I was so worried," she sobs, burying her face into his chest. He holds his hands in the air as if to show me he's not touching her. "When you didn't come home, and then you didn't pick up the phone, I thought maybe... maybe something happened, like it did to my brothers."

He seems to weaken at her words and places one arm around her shoulder, patting her gently. I roll my eyes and open a spreadsheet to try and block out the awful acting. She places her hands on his face and stares intently into his eyes. "Thank God, you're okay. I wouldn't know what to do without you."

"Take his keys and check his other businesses?" I suggest, not looking up from my laptop.

"Meli," he mutters with a hint of warning.

"I reported them missing last night," Jolene sniffles, taking his hand and sitting at his desk. He

# ARTHUR

crouches down. "The police said they'd look into it, seeing as I haven't seen either of them for days."

"That's good. It gets the ball rolling."

She nods, sniffling again until he reaches for a tissue and hands it to her. "I can't have a funeral," she whispers, releasing another fresh round of sobs.

"They might find them," I suggest.

"They won't," she sniffles.

"How do you know?"

"Because they're long gone, Melanie," she snaps.

"Meli," I correct. "The police can do all sorts these days. Forensics might find traces."

"In acid?" snaps Jolene, rolling her eyes like I'm stupid. She turns her attention back to Arthur. "Can you accompany me later? I have a business meeting about one of the apartment blocks."

"Of course," he says, standing to check his diary. "What time?"

"Eight."

"Eight?" I repeat. "In the evening? Who arranges meetings that late?"

Jolene stands, kissing Arthur on each cheek. "Thank you. I'll text you the details."

Once she's gone, I glare at Arthur, who is busy texting on his phone. "She's putting that on," I snap. "The woman deserves an Oscar for that performance."

"I know," he mutters, not looking at me.

"So, why didn't you call her out?"

"Because, Melanie," he grins, placing his phone on his desk and coming over to me, "liars trip themselves up if they think everyone believes them."

"What is she lying about exactly?"

He shrugs, taking my hand and pulling me to stand. "I don't know just yet, but I'll find out."

"By having evening meetings?" I ask, using air quotes.

He laughs, wrapping his arms around me. "How bad are the ribs?" he asks, kissing me.

"Very bad."

"What if I do all the work?" he suggests, reaching over to lock the office door.

---

We shower together in the office bathroom. I love these moments when we're alone and he isn't attached to his mobile. He's not distracted, unless you count the way he keeps looking at me like he wants to eat me all over again. "Will we ever live like this?" I ask, wrapping myself in a towel.

"Aren't we already?"

"I mean spending time together. Maybe not at the office," I laugh, "but, yah know, like normal couples."

"You want marriage, kids, a beautiful home?" he teases.

"Not kids," I scoff, and he frowns. My playful smile disappears. "You want kids?" I ask. He just doesn't seem the type, so I assumed he felt the same as me, and I'm pretty sure I mentioned I didn't want them when we spoke on the rooftop that time.

"You don't?" he asks, frowning. I shake my head. "I didn't think you were serious before. Why not?"

I shrug, beginning to dry myself. "I don't know what I have to offer another human that will depend on me for everything."

"You have loads to offer," he reassures me. "You'd be a great mum."

I pull on my clothes. "Maybe so, but it's not something I want."

## ARTHUR

I can't deny Meli's floored me with her confession about not wanting kids. But I have other things to deal with right now, like the fact Jolene mentioned acid when it's not something we'd told her.

I meet Albert, Tommy, and Charlie at the boxing gym we own. Charlie runs it, so I'm not surprised to find him in the ring sparring with a younger lad. He pats him on the back and tells him to take a break. "So," he says, leaning on the ropes, "what was so important you had to interrupt my day?"

I grab his ankle and pull his feet from under him. He crashes to the mat, and Albert laughs. "Remem-

## NICOLA JANE

ber who you're talking to, little brother," I say, patting his stomach hard. "Jolene was snooping around my office earlier," I tell them. "She used the keys from my house to let herself in."

"Why?" asks Tommy.

"I'm not sure, but she said something interesting. She mentioned her brothers being put into acid."

Albert frowns. "We didn't tell her that."

"Exactly, we wanted to spare her the details, so how does she know?"

My mobile rings and I step away to answer. "Mr. Chai, how are you?" We're about to sign the deal on his hotel. It's in central London, a tidy little spot near our casino. It'll make the perfect location should we want to expand, but the deal's taken me a long time to work out with Mr. Chai being a pain in my arse.

"I'm sorry to do this to you, Arthur," he begins, and I hold my breath, "but I've had a better offer."

"What?" I snap. "By who?"

"It doesn't matter. They've offered my original price."

"Chai, we both know it isn't worth that. Who the fuck would give you that?"

"I'm sorry." He disconnects, and I stare at my phone.

"Chai just pulled out," I tell my brothers.

Albert groans, covering his face. "What now? He's been busting our balls for a deal for months."

# ARTHUR

"He's had a better offer."

"Let me call my guy and see if we can find out what the fuck's going on," says Albert.

When he returns from the gym office, his face tells me I'm not going to be happy. "I think we underestimated our Jolene Hall," he mutters.

I slam my hands against the wall. "Fuck."

"She must have found the file in your office."

I call her, and she answers with a sing-song hello. "Meet me at my office in the next ten minutes," I hiss.

"It doesn't work like that, boo. I have a meeting to sign a very important contract. I'll pop along after." She disconnects, and I have to take a few deep breaths to calm myself.

"Do we kill her slow?" asks Tommy.

"Very," I mutter.

When I get back to the office, there's no sign of Meli, but Rosey is spinning in my office chair. "Where's Meli?" I ask.

"She had to pop to the post office or something. I'm here to take her home."

"I can take her home," I snap.

She holds her hands up in defence. "Okay, chill. What's crawled up your arse?"

"Did you know Meli doesn't want kids?" I blurt.

Rosey shrugs. "I don't blame her. She probably regrets what happened between her and Grim."

"Why would that make her not want kids?"

"Because I think she regretted the abortion right after, and she's regretted it every day since. It was a hard time for her."

I let her words sink in, forcing my face to stay neutral. "I guess," I mutter. "Look, you go. I'll bring her home soon. I still have some work for her to do."

Rosey jumps up. "Okay, whatever."

I wait patiently for Meli to return. When she does, she looks relaxed, but I'm in a mood and I know I should just take her home before I say something I regret, but I'm too worked up. "The whole kid thing," I begin, and she rolls her eyes, "is it just because you don't want them with me, or you don't want them at all?"

"At all," she confirms.

"You've never wanted them, not with anyone else?"

She looks confused. "No."

"Not even with Grim?" I snap.

She eyes me for a second. "Not even with Grim."

"Is that why you got rid of his kid?" I shout. "Or was it out of spite because he loved your sister?"

A range of emotions pass over her face . . . hurt, disappointment, and anger. "You're a dick," she mutters, grabbing her bag. Albert comes in, with Jolene right behind him.

Meli goes to leave, but Jolene puts her arm across the door. "You need to be here for this part."

# ARTHUR

"I really don't," snaps Meli.

Jolene shuts the door, so she can't leave. "What the fuck are you doing?" I snap.

"She's got her security waiting downstairs," Albert warns.

"I don't give a fuck," I yell. "You've lost your mind if you think you can walk into my office and take control."

"That's the problem with you men," Jolene begins. "You all think I'm incapable. Like a woman can't run business as good as you men."

"If this is some bullshit talk about feminism, I'm not interested," I snap. "I want my deal back with Chai."

"We all have to get used to disappointment, Arthur. I planned on dragging this out a lot longer. I wanted you to fall for me naturally, but you've forced my hand with all your snooping antics. I mean, really, smashing up Donnie's bar first thing?" She shakes her head like she's the one disappointed.

"You think because your brothers died and you inherited a few businesses, you're ready to take on the world?" I ask, laughing. "You can't handle it."

"Oh, Arthur, Arthur, Arthur," she says with a heavy sigh. "I've been running the show all along. The 'man' you've been looking for is me."

I let her words sink in, waiting for her to crack a smile and tell me she's joking. But she doesn't.

# NICOLA JANE

"Bullshit," I mutter. All the pieces begin to click into place and the realisation that she's been running things all along hits me like a freight train.

"It was easier for you to believe I was having a threesome with the Palmer brothers rather than running them. You were so easily fooled. You believed the gossip rather than checking the facts. It makes you sloppy."

"You had your brothers killed," mutters Albert. "That's how you knew about the acid."

I pull my gun from my drawer, and Jolene smiles. "I wouldn't if I was you."

"You're not the one with the gun," I say.

"I don't need one," she says confidently. "If anything happens to me, your lovely ma pays the price."

I pause, my hand resting on the cold metal. "What?"

"You heard right. Your brothers really shouldn't have left her alone today."

"You fuckin—"

"Relax, she's happy having tea and biscuits with my men, playing dominoes, and gambling, I might add. But she's a dear."

I slam the drawer closed and let out a roar, turning my back on her and clutching my head in my hands. "If anything happens to her, I'll kill every single one of you," I growl.

"What exactly do you want?" Albert asks.

# ARTHUR

"I'm getting to that. Let's all calm down and have a talk," she says.

I take a few calming breaths before nodding to indicate I'm calmer. She takes a seat, and we all do the same. "First of all, I want to apologise for the Chai deal. I was looking through your paperwork. You really shouldn't leave that stuff lying around." I glance at Meli, knowing it wasn't me who left it out. She looks down at the ground. "We have the chance to rule London," she continues, "together."

I pull my eyes from Meli. "What?"

"Me and you. You and I," she says, grinning. "We can join forces and continue running businesses together."

"I don't take partners," I mutter.

"As your wife," she adds.

I laugh, and so does Albert. "You've lost your mind if you think I'll marry you. You killed your brothers to get your hands on their business."

"Unfortunate, but if you knew them, you'd understand."

"I did know them," I hiss. "You don't kill family."

"Unless they were scumbags who abused you most of your life."

I inhale sharply, glancing at Meli. I wondered how no one at the club could have known what Ripper was doing, and here I was drinking and doing business with Max and Leon, and they were possibly just like him. "Don't get caught in the details," she continues. "Focus on my offer."

I give my head a shake to clear the ache I'm getting. "Why would I agree to that?" I ask. "I have a girlfriend."

Jolene looks at Meli, smirking. "Which is exactly why you're doing this. If you don't agree, I'll have her killed." I stare wide-eyed. "And if you still don't agree, I'll move through your family one by one."

"This is ridiculous," says Albert, throwing his hands in the air in frustration. "What's to stop him killing you once we have Ma back safe?"

"What do you think the cops will say when I suggest you killed my brothers?" she asks, grinning.

I sigh. "With no evidence, how the fuck will you do that?"

"I'm very creative. Just look at this from the outside," she continues. "I'll tell the police you promised to marry me and then killed my brothers so you could get your hands on their business."

Albert scoffs. "That'll never stick."

She arches her brow. "Are you willing to find out? Arthur will spend forever in prison, I'll have already wiped you and your family away, and guess who'll take over."

"You're fucking crazy," he mutters.

"I prefer clever," she counters. "Besides, the cops will dig through everything you own, every business, every employee, every dodgy deal, and every bit of dirty money you clean through your clubs."

"What if I kill you before you get a chance to do any of that?" I ask.

"I'll be getting a phone call every day to check I'm alive and well. The day I don't answer, a price will be put on Albert's head."

"No. No. Just fucking no," snaps Albert. "Kill me now because he isn't marrying you."

"Is that right?" asks Jolene, staring at me. Meli has her head down, so I can't read her emotions. "It's just a call away and your ma is gone. Then another call and Albert will follow."

I pinch the bridge of my nose, trying to think through my options. "Fuck her, Arthur, she's not doing this. She can't have me killed. I'll have her killed first."

"Let me think," I mutter, standing and pacing.

"After Albert, there's a list to work down, and I'm not short of people," says Jolene.

"Kill us all. I'd rather we were all dead than he marries you," snaps Albert.

"You don't have a choice," mutters Meli, finally looking at me. She clears her throat. "You don't have a choice."

"There's always a choice," I say.

She shakes her head. "Not a good one."

"I need a minute," I say. "Let me talk to Meli."

"I'm not leaving. Do your talking here," says Jolene.

"Please," I growl. "If I agree to this, what's a few minutes to say goodbye?"

Jolene sighs but stands. "Fine. Two minutes."

I wait for her and Albert to leave before pulling Meli to stand. There's still hurt in her eyes, and I hate myself for it. "I'm sorry I said all that to you. I had no right. I was angry when I found out you'd aborted the baby, but I know you had your reasons, and they're none of my business. It's no excuse, but I was angry about Jolene taking my deal and I took it out on you."

"You have to do what she wants," she says, not addressing my apology.

"I can't lose you."

"And you can't lose your mum and Albert. She's got you exactly where she wants you."

I cup her face in my hands. "I fucking hate her," I whisper angrily. "Why aren't you angry?"

"I am, Arthur. But something told me you'd never be mine, not truly. And she's right, you'd have so much power if you joined forces."

I place my finger over her lips. "Don't fucking put a positive spin on this, Meli. It's tearing me up inside."

A tear rolls down her cheek, the only sign to show me she feels something. "I don't want to let her see us upset," she whispers. "She gets a kick from it."

## ARTHUR

"I'll find a way. I promise. I'll get out of this before we hear wedding bells." She nods, and more tears roll down her cheeks. "No one tells me what to do. She'll die for crossing me." I wipe her cheeks. "I have no right, but you're mine, Amelia. I can't stand to see you with anyone else. Just wait for me to sort this out and I'm all yours. Okay?"

"Okay," she whispers.

Jolene and Albert come back in. "So, are the goodbyes out the way?" she asks, grinning.

"Seriously?" yells Albert. "You're gonna agree to this shitshow?"

"I can't lose you, Bert," I tell him. "I can't risk it."

"So, what, we just hand everything over like fucking puppy dogs?"

"What choice do I have?" I growl. "Ma is with them now. I can't protect her any other way."

He turns to Jolene. "I might have underestimated you, but you've certainly underestimated me if you think I'll let this go ahead."

# Chapter Sixteen

MELI

I don't cry as Albert takes me home. We sit in silence most of the way until I can't stand it any longer. "What are we going to do?"

"We?" he repeats, smirking. "We're a 'we' now?"

"Rosey could go and get your ma, then Arthur can kill Jolene."

"That all sounds neat and tidy, Meli, but I don't think it'll work."

I scowl at his condescending tone. "Didn't speaking to women like that get you into this mess in the first place?" I snap. "I'm trying to think of something to help."

# ARTHUR

He sighs. "You're right, sorry. It's been a long morning." He pulls into the car park at the clubhouse. "I'll let Mav know the situation."

I follow him to Mav's office, indicating for Rosey, who is watching television in the main room, to follow. The men are not pushing us out of this. When Mav and Rosey are up to date, he turns to me. "Are you okay?"

I shrug, then I feel a familiar lump in my throat but swallow it down. Tears won't save Arthur. "He said he'll come up with a plan."

"Rosey, can't you find out if there's a hit on any of us?" asks Albert. "She could be lying."

"I can try, but it's not like we have a directory of hitmen and women. She could have hired anyone from anywhere in the world."

"I'll keep my eyes and ears open," I say, and when Albert looks confused, I add, "She didn't fire me from the office. I'm still gonna show up for work every day."

"Good idea," says Albert. "I'm gonna hire a housekeeper too. We need as many insiders as we can find."

"I'll do it," I offer. "She doesn't know who works for Arthur and what they do. I'll just tell her that's how I started dating him, through him hiring me."

"Are you sure? That could get messy if you've got to see them together," says Mav.

"I need to feel like I'm doing something. I'll call by later this evening. The worst she can do is send me away."

"I'll try and locate your mother," offers Rosey.

"I'll put someone on you, Meli. Please don't go off on your own," says Mav, and I nod. I don't intend to now I know there's a price on my head. "Rosey, you can do the honours, splitting time with Viking."

"Really? New guy?" she cries. "He's gonna stand out."

"Dice told me to bring you in on more club business, so don't make me regret it," he snaps.

---

I managed to get Mama B to put a bucket of cleaning supplies together, so it looks as though I do this sort of thing regular. She even found me an apron.

Rosey drops me off at Arthur's house, and as I head up the driveway, nerves overtake my body. I stop and take a deep breath. I can do this. I have to, for Arthur. I'm relieved to see the lights off and no one home. Albert gave me the key and alarm code, so I go right in, jumping into the role as housekeeper.

I take the bedroom first, smiling when I see his unmade bed. I fold the sheets back slightly and plump his pillows, then I go and make a start on the

# ARTHUR

en-suite. Next, I go to the spare room that Jolene is currently staying in. The bed is made, and the windows are open to let in fresh air. There's a bag on the dresser full of expensive makeup. I pick up a pricey bottle of perfume and spritz it, inhaling the sharp, musky scent. I roll my eyes because, of course, she's dripping in good perfume and nice makeup. I open her walk-in wardrobe and scan the rail of expensive brands, noticing there's a lot of new garments with the tags still attached.

I hear the front door open and Arthur shouting hello. He must be wondering why the lights are on, although Albert gave him the heads-up. "It's just me," I shout back, collecting my bucket and heading out the room. I get to the top of the stairs and see Jolene standing behind him. It stops me in my tracks. "Hey. I'm done up here, so I'll make a start in the kitchen."

"Great," mutters Arthur, taking his coat off and hanging it on the hook. Jolene coughs to get his attention and then she turns, indicating she wants him to remove her coat. He does it with an annoyed expression.

"What is this exactly?" asks Jolene.

"Didn't I mention? She does some housekeeping for me," he explains.

"Since when?"

"A few months," he says, shrugging. "I can't remember. Albert sorts out the staff."

"It's seven in the evening, a bit late for cleaning."

"I fit it around the office and my life," I say, heading down the stairs and passing her to go to the kitchen.

She follows. "As long as this isn't a ploy to make my life hell."

I smirk. "Like you're making Arthur's?"

"He might feel like that now, but once he see's how good we are together and how the businesses will flourish, he'll realise I was right."

Anxiety sits heavy in my chest. What if she's correct and he decides he likes the arrangement? "I have to get on," I mutter.

"Fine. If you want to torture yourself and watch him fall in love with me, be my guest. It makes my life more fun. Did you clean my room?" I nod, spraying down the worktops and wiping. Arthur comes in, heading straight for the coffee machine. "What are your duties, exactly?" she asks.

I hesitate, not knowing what to say. It's not something I discussed with Albert. "You've had a housekeeper before, right?" snaps Arthur, looking at her like she's stupid. "She does housekeeping things."

"Great. Can you move my things from the spare bedroom into Arthur's."

# ARTHUR

I falter, almost knocking a glass off the worktop but catching it in time before it topples. "That's not in her job description," Arthur hisses.

"You just said—" Jolene begins, but I cut in.

"It's fine. Of course, I can." I rush off upstairs before Arthur can protest any more. She's probably just testing me, but either way, I can't fall apart. So, I begin gathering her belongings and taking them to Arthur's room, putting her clothes neatly beside his, her perfume next to his aftershave, which I can't resist inhaling, and her toothbrush beside his. Out of all the things I move, it's the toothbrushes that hurt my heart. I stare at them side by side and have the urge to snap them both. Maybe it's because I never got that far.

I feel him behind me and pull my eyes away. "I told Albert this was a stupid idea," he mutters.

"I offered," I say. "I can be the eyes and ears."

"She knows you're more than that to me," he snaps.

"Then it's up to me to convince her I don't feel the same."

"Meli..." He's shaking his head, his expression full of doubt.

I place my hand on his chest. "Let me do this, Arthur. I have to feel like I'm doing something. I can handle Jolene Hall. Trust me to act like a true professional."

## NICOLA JANE

He smiles. "A new line of work?"

I nod. "Maybe Rosey can hire me if I do a good job."

"I should tell you—"

"Wow, you've moved everything already," comes Jolene's voice.

When she gets to the doorway, I mouth the word 'sorry' to Arthur before slapping him hard in the face. He growls, gripping his cheek. "Fuck," he hisses.

"I told you to leave me alone," I yell. "If I didn't need the money, I'd tell you where to shove your job."

"Ouch," smirks Jolene. "I hope you weren't getting hands-on with the maid."

"I think we're clear where we all stand," growls Arthur, storming out the bathroom.

I grip my sore hand to my chest, forcing myself not to cry. "I'll finish up downstairs."

## ARTHUR

My head's a fucking mess. My cheek burns after Meli's little display for Jolene, and all I can think about is how the fuck I'm gonna get out of this. I'll lose people who mean so much to me if I pull out of this. She's made it clear she won't stop her killing spree until everyone I love is dead, and the only answer I can come up with is to hand it all over to her. It's an idea that Albert will hate, and honestly, I

# ARTHUR

don't even think she'll go for it. I don't think it's my business Jolene is after. She wants to stand by my side and feel the power I hold.

Jolene is in the kitchen opening a bottle of red wine, Meli is stacking the dishwasher, and I stand in the doorway thinking how crazy this scene is. The woman I love and the woman I despise are in the same room. I shake my head, laughing to myself. "Wine?" asks Jolene. I shake my head. "Martha, get him a whiskey."

"Her name is Meli, as you damn well know," I snap, "and I don't want a whiskey."

"You need to loosen up. It's our first night together as a couple."

I roll my eyes. "We're not a couple."

"We're getting married, of course, we are. Speaking of which, my vicar called, and he can fit us in as early as next week."

I glare at her, and Meli does too, we're both shocked. "You can't organise a wedding in a week," mutters Meli. She glances at me, and I can see the panic in her eyes. How the hell am I going to come up with a plan in a week?

"I have a dress. I've dreamed of this day for years, so I'm ready to go."

"Don't you think it'll look suspicious?" I ask. "You're getting married right after your brothers are killed."

## NICOLA JANE

"The cops don't care about Leon and Max, we both know that," she replies, rolling her eyes.

"I don't want the focus on me," I snap. "Is this your plan going into action, Jolene, because I won't go down for something I didn't do."

"Blah, blah, blah. This conversation is getting boring. Face the fact that we're getting married and you're not getting out of it."

"I have to go," Meli announces. "Have a great evening."

I have to fight everything in me not to stop her leaving. I've killed men with my bare hands, but being alone with this crazy bitch feels like the scariest thing I've done. "You too," I mutter.

"We'll have a great night, won't we?" adds Jolene, winking.

Meli forces a smile. "Let me know if there's anything I can help with." She pauses and frowns then gets flustered, realising what she's said. "I meant the wedding. Anything I can help with on the wedding." She grabs her things and rushes for the door. I can't help but smile. She's got a way with words that's all Meli, and no one can make me smile like she does.

"She thinks I don't know what she's up to, what you're all up to," Jolene says, draining her glass of wine.

"What's that?"

# ARTHUR

"You're thinking of ways out of this." She places her glass on the side. "But let me tell you, Arthur, there is none."

"Why are you doing this?"

"Imagine how powerful we'll be," she says, grinning. "We'll run the streets together, take over any area we want until we run it all."

"You remind me of someone," I tell her, and she comes closer, running her hand over my chest. I remove it. "When I was rising up through the ranks, I worked for Big Tommy Shelton. He talked just like you, about taking over London. And I used to think he was on to something until I realised how big London was. No one can run London single-handed."

"That's why I have you. Unfortunately, the men in our world still see females as weak. I need you beside me to make them take notice."

"And that's where you're going wrong. If you wanna take over more areas, they can't see you coming."

"Just like you didn't," she says, grinning. She grabs my cock through my trousers. "How does it feel to be owned by a woman?"

I smirk. "Meli will always own me, Jolene, no matter how hard you try."

"Yet you'll be marrying me, sleeping with me, fathering my children."

I laugh. "You're deluded. There's no way I'm going near you again."

She narrows her eyes. "Oh, but you are, Arthur. Because if you don't, I'll wipe that little bitch from your life completely." She begins to unbutton my shirt. "And I'll make you watch."

---

I wake with a start, sitting up and looking around the room. Jolene stirs, and I get out of bed before she demands a repeat of last night. I go to the spare room to use the shower. I scrub myself like it'll somehow wash away the feel of her on my skin. If this is my life now, I'm fucked.

Albert is downstairs making coffee. "What are you doing here?" I mutter, slipping on my jacket.

"Thought I'd check in on you. That's allowed, right? Or are there more rules?"

"Don't start, Bert. My head is fucked and I'm about to break. I had no choice, you know deep down I don't."

"I've got Rosey on it," he says in a whisper. "She's trying to find the hitman."

"And how the hell will she take down someone who's trained to do the same job as her?"

"I don't know, Arthur, I'm just trying to get us out of this mess."

I take his coffee from him. "Just say it," I snap. "You know you want to."

# ARTHUR

"If you already know, then why do I need to say it?"

I shrug. "Suit yourself." I head for the door.

"Fine, if you hadn't slept with her, this wouldn't have happened."

I laugh, turning back to face him. "You think my cock is that magical, she became obsessed? She doesn't want me for that." I take a deep breath. "But she wants what I have, the power, the money, the businesses."

"I told you not to do business with the Clifton brothers. You got too greedy and now look. She wouldn't even know you if it weren't for them."

I rush towards him, backing him up against the wall. "You might have to clean up some of the mess I make, but don't fucking dare tell me I'm bad at business. I got us this far."

"Yeah, and then you fucked it all up for pussy."

"What's that supposed to mean?"

"You took your eye off the ball, Arthur. You were too focussed on Meli to see what was going on."

"You didn't see this either," I yell. "How the fuck was I meant to know Jolene was a crazy psycho? She played the dumb bitch act well."

"I'm warning you now, brother. We're not going down. I'd rather kill our entire family before I let her walk away with what we built."

## NICOLA JANE

I cup the back of his neck and rest my forehead against his. "I'll find a way, Bert. I always do."

---

Meli arrives to the office and smiles when she sees me. My heart feels heavy at what I'm about to do, but I have no choice. It kept me up all night thinking about it. I'm gonna hurt her too much if I don't make it easier for us both now. I wait until she drops her bag by her desk and comes towards me before I stand and hold up my hand. She stops, immediately looking confused. "Jolene could walk in," I mutter. "I don't need to give her any more ammunition."

"Oh god, you're really gonna do this," she almost whispers.

"How do you know what I'm thinking all the time?" I ask, gently running my thumb along her jaw and cupping her face. "Don't make this hard."

She steps back, inhales, and fixes me with a hard stare. "I sort of expected it," she says, her voice void of emotion. "You don't need to say the words. I get it."

"I can't find a way out while you're in my head," I explain.

She nods. "Okay."

"Let me explain, Meli, please," I beg.

"To make yourself feel better?" she asks coldly.

# ARTHUR

"No," I say on a sigh, "but how can I keep you hanging on when I don't know if I'll even get out of this? I felt so fucking dirty and ashamed this morning. The guilt alone will rip me apart if we try and keep what we have."

"Jesus, it's been less than twenty-four hours and you're choosing her."

"No," I snap. "I'm not fucking choosing her. I don't have a damn choice, that's the whole problem. She's using you as a threat for everything, Meli. Holding you over my head like a damn toy. If you end up dead because of me, I'll never forgive myself. Your brother will never forgive me."

"It's for the best," she says, nodding and going back to her desk.

"And I can't feel the amount of guilt I do when we're still holding on."

"Exactly," she agrees. "You need to feel free to fuck her without thinking you're cheating."

"That's not what I mean," I mutter.

"Isn't it? You're dumping me so you can fuck her and not feel bad. Job done, consider me dumped."

"Meli, you're making this hard."

She clutches her hands over her heart and gives a sad expression. "Oh, I'm sorry," she says, her tone dripping in sarcasm. "I didn't mean to make you feel worse. I'll make you feel better, shall I? Maybe I can fuck someone, move on quickly, will that help ease your conscience?"

I bite my inner cheek to stop me pinning her against the wall and reminding her exactly why it wouldn't be good to taunt me with jealousy. "You do whatever you need to." I force the words out. "I just needed to make things easier all round." I go back to my desk, forcing myself to sit down and open my laptop. "I'll send your final wage later today."

"Final wage?" she repeats.

I look over to her. "Yes. You can't keep working here."

She laughs. "Not a fucking chance are you firing me. This is my job and I'm good at it, and unless you want the hassle of Hadley taking you to court for unfair dismissal, I'd stay quiet."

"You know it's going to be hard to watch me and Jolene together," I mutter.

"Hard for me, or hard for you?" she asks.

The office door opens and Jolene walks in looking like an advert for Versace. "Good morning. You were up and gone early," she says, striding over to my desk and kissing me. "Morning sex is my absolute fave."

"Shocking, so is Arthur's," says Meli, mocking Jolene's screechy tone.

Jolene smirks, pressing her lips against mine again before turning to look at Meli. "Maybe I tired him

# ARTHUR

out," she says thoughtfully, and I groan. This is the exact thing I wanted to avoid.

Meli grins wider, leaning her chin on her hands. "He's an all-night kind of guy, so I find it hard to believe. Is your stamina slipping, Art?" she asks, glancing at me.

"Stop," I snap, and they both look at me. "This stops now."

Jolene shrugs. "So, wedding plans, I'm going shopping to get some last-minute things. I need a list from you of all the people we need to invite."

"Like?" I ask, irritated.

"Like all the important business associates."

"All the men she needs to impress, silly," adds Meli.

"Exactly," Jolene confirms, ignoring the sarcasm in Meli's voice. "And family, of course."

"Shit, haven't you lost yours?" Meli asks. "That's gonna be awkward. Arthur's side will be full and yours will be empty."

"Maybe you can sit on my side to fill it. Your arse is a good size," snaps Jolene.

Meli laughs. "I'd rather be dead than come to this sham of a wedding."

"That can be arranged," Jolene says. "But I'd rather not kill you just yet, I'm enjoying pissing you off too much."

# NICOLA JANE

I stand abruptly. "I have a meeting to go to. When I come back, I want you both to be gone."

# Chapter Seventeen

MELI

I roll my eyes as they both leave the office. I just told him I'm not going anywhere, and I meant it, because despite his words, there's no way I'm giving up on him. He's mine, and I'm fighting for him.

I call Rosey and meet her for lunch. She looks tired and stressed. "Are you okay?"

She shrugs. "All this stuff with Arthur is getting to me," she admits, and I frown. Nothing gets to Rosey. "It's such a mess, and it hurts my head trying to think of ways to get rid of that scheming bitch."

"Tell me about it. Any luck on the other hitman or woman?"

She shakes her head. "No one openly talks about this stuff. I can't just rock up to some HQ and demand a list of killers and clients. It'll take time, and from what Albert tells me, there's no time because she's set the wedding date for Friday."

I nod. "Yep. She's ready to go."

Rosey gives me a pitying smile. "How are you feeling?"

"More determined," I admit. "She's not getting him. Even if they make it down the aisle, she's not keeping him. We'll find a way."

"Is he . . . yah know, sleeping with her?"

I shrug even though I know he is. "Maybe. She's dropping threats all over the place. She mentioned having a baby with him."

Rosey gasps. "That's the ultimate trap. If he has a kid, he can't just walk away."

"Don't," I whisper, feeling the ache in my heart. "I can't think about it."

"Didn't you tell him you don't want kids?" she asks, making me feel worse. I nod. "Does he?" I nod again and bury my face in my hands. "He wants them with you, Meli, not her. Let's not get ahead. Maybe we can slip the morning-after pill into her coffee," she adds, and we laugh.

"Or arsenic?" I suggest.

"Mav is working on helping him too. We'll come up with a way."

"I know," I mutter. "I just feel like she's got every angle covered."

# ARTHUR

When I return to the office, Arthur is back. I sit at my desk without a word, and I feel his eyes fixed on me. "This won't work, you working here," he says.

"Look," I say firmly, "no pressure, okay. Let's take a step back and remove all pressure. Who do you love?"

"You."

"How many kids do you want?"

"You don't want kids," he replies.

"If I did, how many?"

"As many as you'll allow."

"Favourite honeymoon destination?"

"Maldives."

"Think of those answers. Every time you want to give up, think of those answers. You love me, we'll get married and honeymoon in the Maldives, and we'll make a start on the babies there."

He smiles. "Babies?"

"Maybe two. A boy and a girl, if possible."

"You want kids?"

"With you," I whisper. "Only with you." He nods, a look of calm passing over his face. "So, no pressure at all. Do what you have to do to get through this until we find a way out. Which we will."

"Thank you," he murmurs.

## NICOLA JANE

"I've made a start on the guestlist," I announce, holding up a notepad.

"You don't need to do that," he says, looking uncomfortable.

"We're in this together, right? If I hang around long enough, I might find some information that could help."

---

After leaving the office, I make my way to Arthur's house again. This time, Jolene is home. She's in the kitchen cooking, and two men are with her. They all look at me as I enter. "Would you like me to start upstairs?" I ask, smiling politely at her guests.

"Who are you?" asks one, grinning.

"She's the maid," Jolene jumps in, looking annoyed.

"Meli," I introduce, seeing as she isn't bothering to.

"Danny. Pleased to meet you. That's my brother, Curtis."

I smile shyly, trying my hardest to look sweet and innocent because my instincts tell me these two clowns will be Jolene's downfall. "I should get on."

"Wait," he rushes after me, catching me as I'm about to head upstairs. "Are you single, married, other?" he asks, laughing at his own joke.

"Very single. You?"

## ARTHUR

"Same. Maybe we could go out for a drink some time?"

I bite my lower lip, and his eyes fall there. "Sure, but I don't date men I don't know alone. Do you mind if I bring my friend?"

He nods eagerly. "Of course. I'll bring Curtis."

"It's best you don't tell your boss," I whisper, nodding to the kitchen where Jolene is chatting to his brother. "She hates me."

The front door opens, and Arthur stops when he sees Danny. He closes the door, keeping his eyes on us. "No problem," Danny replies. "Let me take your number, and I'll text you to work out a date we can all make."

I nod, handing him my phone. "What's going on?" asks Arthur.

Danny inputs his number to my phone before calling his own. He hands it back, completely ignoring Arthur. "Speak soon." He winks, then goes back into the kitchen.

Arthur grabs my upper arm and marches me up the stairs. He doesn't stop until we're in his bedroom, and he slams the door. "Explain."

"He asked me on a date," I begin to explain.

"What?" he growls. "Well, you moved on quick. Jesus, Meli. One minute, you're telling me to picture us and kids, and the next, you're handing your number to one-half of the chuckle brothers."

I smile, pressing my lips together. He looks hot when he's jealous. "I'm taking Rosey. I think the chuckle brothers could be where we get our information from. They're not going to want to work under you. There must be something they'll give away that we can use."

Arthur grins. "You're going on a date for me?"

I laugh. "Okay, smart arse, it sounds crazy, but I have a hunch."

He pushes me against the wall, cupping my face in his hands. "Well, if it's a hunch, I'll allow it." He kisses me until my toes curl. "But be careful. These guys are working directly under her. They could be dangerous, and I don't want you getting hurt. Speak to Mav about it. I need to get downstairs before she realises I'm home."

"She's cooking dinner for you."

He groans. "Christ, she might have poisoned it."

"Wait until she eats first," I warn, grinning. "I love you."

His smile is huge, and I feel myself blushing, realising it's the first time I've said the words out loud. The scariest thing is, I didn't even know they were there. They just slipped out so naturally. "You love me?" he repeats.

I try to step around him. "Well, it's no big deal, so let's not get all weird."

# ARTHUR

He pulls me back, kissing me again. "I love you too, Angel. You have no idea how hard this is. It's killing me."

"I had to make your bed," I mutter. "I could smell her perfume all over the sheets."

He presses his forehead against mine. "Don't think about it."

"It's hard not to." I take a deep breath. "We'll find a way to get you out of this. In the meantime, think of an excuse to keep her away from you. Tell her I've given you an STD."

He laughs. "Okay."

I nod in satisfaction and pull him in for one last kiss. "Go, before she finds us."

---

I get back to the club and go straight for Mav's office, telling Rosey to follow me. "I have us a double date," I announce.

Mav frowns. "I'm married."

"Me and Rosey," I say, rolling my eyes.

"What's that got to do with me? And Arthur's gonna lose his mind."

"Arthur knows, it's to help him. I met Danny and Curtis tonight. Danny took a shine to me, asked me on a date. I think we can get something on her from them, but Arthur told me to run it by you."

## NICOLA JANE

"We could kill them. Once she's lost those two, then what?" asks Rosey.

"No," snaps Mav, glaring at her. "Absolutely not. Meli isn't going on your little killing spree, Harley Quinn, so forget that idea."

I laugh. "I don't think we'll need to. We can get all the information we need by using our charm."

"Okay. Good work. I'll have to put someone on you," says Mav.

"Mav, you can't do that. It'll blow everything. They're not going to open up if—"

"Fine," says Rosey, taking me by the arm and pulling me from the office. "Whatever."

I scowl at her. "What are you doing? These guys can't be jumpy, or they won't slip-up."

"First of all, how long have we been doing this? You know as well as I do, he'll never let us out without his eyes and ears following. Secondly, since when have we ever followed club protocol? Set the date up and we'll tell Mav the wrong day and time."

I grin, pulling out my mobile. "On it."

## ARTHUR

I stare at the steak and salad Jolene prepared and cooked. "It looks good," I tell her, because it really does, "thanks."

"Has a woman ever cooked for you before?" she asks, pouring herself a glass of wine.

# ARTHUR

I shake my head. "But I'm not going to talk about my private life with you, Jolene."

She shrugs. "Fair enough, I don't blame you."

"Why were your thugs in my home tonight?" I was prepared to throw them out after I left Meli, but they'd already gone.

She pauses, mid-chew. "Thugs?"

"The Palmer brothers."

"They're not thugs, Arthur, and if I heard right, you and your brothers started out just like them and look at you now. Do people refer to you as thugs?"

"The difference is, when my brothers and I were climbing our way to the top, we did it with dignity and grace. We didn't take down men who could become alliances."

"Is that what you would have been, Arthur? Even without my brothers beside me?"

"Your brothers were never beside you, they were in front. Not because they were men, but because they worked to get there. You were younger, it's the luck of the draw, but you didn't work your way up to become like them. You cut them out and took what was theirs. So, no, I wouldn't have worked with you having found out how you got there. I would have if you'd worked for it."

"You have no idea what I went through to get here," she says.

"Then tell me."

# NICOLA JANE

"They never listened. They never gave me a chance."

"Boo-fucking-hoo. There are other ways to become good at what you do, even setting up on your own. You could have still signed your goons and gone out alone."

"They'd have killed me."

"You're not stupid, Jolene. You took me on, so I have no doubt you could have given us all a run for our money. At least we would have respected you."

She drops her fork on the table. "Bullshit. I'd never get the same respect as a man in this world, we both know it. I don't want to talk about this anymore. Let's talk about our wedding and how many children we plan on having."

"Zero with you," I scoff.

She scowls. "Maybe you need inspiration. Maybe I should show a video of your ex being fucked by my goons?" I stand abruptly, and she smirks. "Touched a nerve?"

"If they lay a finger on her, I'll kill you all, no matter what the consequences."

She sighs dreamily. "See, that's the sort of man I want. Someone who'd do anything, even risk his own brother. Now, I'll go and shower and get ready for bed. Join me."

She marches off, and I pull out my phone, calling Meli. She doesn't pick up, and I growl angrily. Her

# ARTHUR

voicemail message cuts in. "Meli, whatever you do, don't arrange to go on a date with the Palmer brothers. It's not safe. I'll explain tomorrow."

---

Jolene lays against me, gently stroking her fingers up and down my chest. I grit my teeth in agitation and sit up, causing her to remove herself from me. "I'm fertile right now," she says, sounding pleased as she lies back down to get comfortable.

"You make my skin crawl."

"You couldn't tell with the way you just fucked me." She sounds smug, and I shake my head in disgust. "Don't be too hard on yourself. I'm your fiancée, you don't have to feel guilty for enjoying it. Besides, it'll get easier with time."

I scrub my hands over my tired face. "Why me?" I mutter.

"Why did I choose to marry you?"

"No, why me at all? Why have you dragged me into all this? Why was I your target? I was getting my life on track and you just—"

"That's your problem, Arthur. You let your guard down because you were too busy trying to get your office girl to fuck you."

"Christ, you sound like Albert." I get up from the bed and head for the shower. She goes to follow, and

# NICOLA JANE

I shake my head. "No. Don't bother." I feel sick to the deepest depths of my stomach. It's all so out of hand, and I feel so fucking powerless. I decide that if there's no plan in place by end of the day tomorrow, I'm going to kill them all, every last one of them. Meli will have to go into lockdown at the clubhouse, along with Albert and the rest of my family. I think of Ma and get the urge to throw up. I rest my forehead against the cool bathroom tiles. I have to face the fact I might not be able to save her too. I slam my fist into the wall, growling in frustration. I can't wait to make Jolene fucking bleed.

# Chapter Eighteen

MELI

"So, Mav thinks the date is tomorrow night," I tell Rosey, slipping my heels off my feet and holding them in my hands as we creep through the clubhouse. A few of the brothers are around, but they don't pay any attention to us, and Grim and Mav went out an hour ago, so when Danny texted me, suggesting a date, I snapped up the chance.

"Great, hopefully, it'll give us time to get what we need before he finds out we've left the club."

"You don't think this looks too keen, a date right away?"

"God, yes, but who cares? This isn't for real."

"I know, I just don't want them to get suspicious. The last thing we need is them turning on us."

# NICOLA JANE

Rosey scoffs. "Please, I live for those moments." I relax a little. At least Rosey can protect us, which will be how I'll explain it to Mav tomorrow when he loses his mind over this. "Before we get there, there're some rules."

"Rules?"

"And you have to take this seriously. We order bottles, stick to beer or something with a small opening so we can see if they slip anything in. Also, don't touch anything. If there's a door, use your sleeve to cover your hand. Don't leave a trace of you in there. Tie your hair up." She hands me a band, and I stare at her like she's lost her mind. "Trust me on this, Meli. Always be prepared."

"I hate tying my hair up."

"But it hurts less if they get aggressive and grab a handful. Tie it low, it's harder for them to get a hold of."

"This is a first date, Rosey, what the hell are you expecting to happen?"

"Jolene's been one step ahead this time, Meli. We just need to be cautious. We beat up the younger brother of these idiots. What if they know that and this is all a ploy to get us there?"

"Oh, great, why didn't you say all this in front of Mav? I'd never have arranged it, especially without him knowing."

# ARTHUR

Rosey grins. "Where would the fun be in that?" I roll my eyes. I am not prepared for this to go south.

"Won't there be cameras?"

She shakes her head. "They don't have cameras, I checked."

We arranged to meet in a small bar on the E15 side of the tracks but very close to the border. It was owned by Jolene's brother, Leon, but I guess it belongs to her now. When we arrive, it's empty apart from the two brothers. Danny smiles when he sees me and comes over, kissing me on the cheek. I force a smile as he places his hand on my lower back and ushers me closer to his brother. "You remember Curtis," he says, and I nod. "Curtis, this is Meli."

"And my friend, Rosey," I add.

Curtis shakes our hands and offers us a seat each at the bar. "What can I get you both?" he asks, going behind the bar.

"Just two bottles of beer, please," says Rosey. "Quiet, isn't it?"

He looks around like he didn't realise and then shrugs. "Sometimes it's like this."

"Do you work here or . . ." Rosey asks.

"We own it." He gives his brother a smile.

"Oh, I thought Jolene did," I say, looking confused.

He narrows his eyes. "Did she say that?"

I nod innocently, hoping my plan to put their boss in a bad light works. "She's always talking about the places she owns. You work for her, right?"

"No," he snaps. "We don't work for anyone."

Danny throws an arm around my shoulder. "Let's not talk about Jolene right now."

"Meli said you were brothers?" asks Rosey.

"Yep," says Danny. "Twins. Non-identical."

"Wow, Meli's a twin too," she replies. "What a coincidence."

They don't seem interested. Instead, Danny takes a seat. "You're both single?"

I nod. "What about you guys?"

"We're too busy for relationships," says Curtis bluntly.

Rosey grins. "Wow, what a thing to bring up on a first date."

He shrugs. "There's no point stringing you along."

"I'm only here for her," Rosey says, rolling her eyes. "But in case you didn't know, you're a terrible charmer."

"We have a roof terrace, why don't we go up there," Danny suggests, breaking the stare-off between Curtis and Rosey.

I smile awkwardly. "If you'd like."

He nods, so we follow him from the bar up some steps that lead out onto the roof. I glance nervously at Rosey. The last time she was on a roof space, she

# ARTHUR

killed Jolene's husband, which probably explains why she doesn't look at all bothered now.

"What happened to you?" Curtis asks, pointing to my fading bruises as we sit.

"She got jumped," says Rosey coldly. "Two cowards."

He presses his lips into a firm line. "You know who did it?"

Danny sighs heavily. "Curtis doesn't mean to be rude, do you?" he says, giving him a pointed look. "Tell us why Jolene hates you," he adds. "You said before that she does."

"I had a thing with Arthur Taylor," I say, and he doesn't look surprised. "She wanted him."

"Were you serious?"

I shake my head. "No, just a casual thing. How long have you worked for her?"

"I told you, we don't work for her," snaps Curtis.

"Then how do you know her?" asks Rosey, "Seeing as you're so adamant she doesn't own your arse."

"We're helping her out," he replies.

"She really talks like . . ." I trail off and bite my lip like I didn't mean to say that. "Never mind."

"No, go on," Curtis pushes.

"Well, she isn't very nice about you. Calls you her dog's bodies, says you do her running around." They exchange a look. "I might be wrong. I just get the impression she really thinks you're beneath her. She doesn't talk to me about it, it's just things I hear when she's on the phone or talking to Arthur."

"I know what you're doing," Curtis announces, a small smile playing on his lips. "It's not going to work."

"I'm not doing anything. I was just telling you how she is."

"You want to cause a divide."

"Why would I?" I ask innocently.

"Because you're Arthur Taylor's woman. Because you're part of The Perished Riders MC. Should I go on?"

I try not to look surprised, and Rosey grins. "I like a man who does his homework."

"Fuck, Curtis, not now," Danny hisses.

"She's not stupid, mate, she's pretending. She already knows you beat the crap out of her, and I'm pretty sure she thought she'd play us tonight to get shit on Jolene, so you weren't gonna get a fuck out of her anyway, but nice try."

Rosey drinks her beer, leaning back casually in her seat. I try to mirror her actions, but I can't hide the fact I'm crapping myself. This suddenly just took a turn, and I can't see a way out as I glance towards the fire exit that seems too far away. "Please tell me she hired you dickheads to be her personal on-call hitmen," she says, her eyes wide with delight.

# ARTHUR

"Because you're going to kill us first?" asks Curtis, throwing his head back in laughter.

Rosey smashes her bottle on the side of her chair, and I flinch in shock, but then Curtis howls in pain. The jagged part of the bottle is in the side of his neck, and it happened so fast, it doesn't quite register as I stand quickly, almost toppling backwards. Danny yells something I don't catch because of my heart beating loudly in my ears.

Rosey releases her hold on the bottle, leaving it in his neck. "Tell me again how you attacked Meli." She goes back to her casual pose, like she didn't do anything out of the ordinary, and I realise this is the first time I've seen her in work mode, and it's terrifying.

"You fucking crazy bitch," yells Danny, rushing to his brother and grabbing the bottle.

"I wouldn't pull that if I was you. He'll bleed out," Rosey mutters like she's bored. "Let's talk."

"Jolene will have you killed," Curtis warns. His brother grabs a blanket lying casually over one of the chairs and wraps it around the bottle to try and stem the slow trickle of blood.

"I want answers," Rosey continues, "and you're going to give them to me."

"You won't get anything from us," yells Danny, watching his brother helplessly.

"I am so disappointed," Rosey continues. "I thought you'd at least pull out a gun. You came unarmed to this date, which tells me you either massively underestimated us as women, or you really thought this was a date." She then pulls out her own gun with a wink.

"You have no idea what you've started," Curtis mutters.

"I knew what I was doing the second I lured your little brother to a flat where Arthur Taylor was waiting for him. Is that what this is all about? Is that why you're helping Jolene to get Arthur back?"

"We're not telling you anything," snaps Danny. "I'm calling an ambulance."

"Let me make you a deal. I'll let you call an ambulance if you answer some questions."

"You don't call the fucking shots," he yells. She throws a glass from the table in his direction, and when he dodges it, she snatches his mobile from his hand. Then, she holds up a second. "I already got your brother's."

"Meli, call an ambulance," he begs. "This is serious."

I stare in disbelief. This guy beat me and left me in the street, and he has the nerve to ask me. "Fuck you."

"Excuse my friend, she's feeling a little upset knowing you beat her and then asked her on a date.

# ARTHUR

Who the hell does that?" asks Rosey. "Meli, don't you think dating's going downhill? You can't trust anyone these days."

"You never know who's behind the mask," I agree.

"I went on a date a few weeks back, and he was married! Wanker," says Rosey, shaking her head.

"This is all fascinating, but can we hurry the fuck up so I can get my brother some help?"

"Who did your boss hire for the hits on Meli and Albert Taylor?" asks Rosey, her voice suddenly serious.

"How the fuck do we know?" snaps Curtis, then he groans in pain.

"You were giving it the big one just then. I thought you had more responsibility in this."

"She's at the top of it all," he growls, "of E15."

Rosey frowns. "She's running the show on her own?"

He nods. "She took over a few months back. Not even her brothers knew."

"And now, she wants to take over Arthur's side of things?"

He shrugs. "She's got bigger plans, I think. She wants his power and the respect he has. She'll only get that by sticking by his side. I think the wedding is for real, and she's probably trying to have his kid too. But she doesn't blink an eye when she orders a kill, and I wouldn't put it past her to wipe out everyone in his life until he only had her."

"Who killed her brothers?" I ask.

"Some guy. She didn't tell us his name, just that he hated her brothers and had wanted to get to them for years. She put a down payment to lure him in, a hotel that was in her married name, because she had no access to funds while her brothers were still alive. She then agreed a price for once they were dead."

I pace, suddenly feeling nauseous. Danny sees it as an opportunity to grab me, pulling me to him. Rosey doesn't seem phased, she simply arches a brow. "What exactly are you going to do with her, you idiot? I have a gun."

"Snap her fucking neck before you've pulled the trigger," he hisses, placing a hand on my forehead while the other holds me tightly around the waist.

"And then what?" she asks with a laugh. "Use her body as a shield?"

I glare at her. "I don't think we should make suggestions, Rosey," I say as calmly as I can because inside, I'm freaking the fuck out.

"Just call a fucking ambulance," he yells.

She stands, shaking her head. "I'm not going to do that, Danny. I just wanted answers, and now, you've ruined it. I've had a really bad week, and this just tops it off." I feel him pulling my head and wonder if it's really possible for him to snap my neck like

# ARTHUR

this. Curtis seems drowsy, his head keeps dropping forward like he can't hold it up.

"I'm sick of women telling us what to do," he shouts. "Curtis, don't go to sleep," he adds, kicking his brother's foot.

"He's bleeding out. You need to release Meli, or I'm not helping you."

"Please," he almost whispers. He holds me tighter, and I gasp. "Don't make me kill her. I just want you to help him."

"You did this yourself," Rosey lectures as she leans forward. I watch in horror as she pulls the bottle from Curtis's neck and blood begins to spurt out to the rhythm of his heart. A painful cry leaves Danny, but he doesn't release me. "You only have minutes, maybe less, before he dies," says Rosey. "You need to cover his wound."

Danny shoves me hard, and I fall onto Rosey. He grabs his brother and pulls him flat to the floor. Rosey wipes the bloody bottle neck where she held it, then passes it to Danny, who automatically takes it without thinking. He frowns, placing it on the ground, then he grabs the blanket again and holds it to his brother's throat. That's when I realise she's just put his prints on the glass.

Rosey takes me by the hand and leads me off the rooftop, slamming the fire exit door and bolting it shut. "Now what?" I ask, my heart still banging hard in my chest.

"Now, we act." She pulls out her phone and dials for the police as we rush down the stairs. "Hello, I need the police! I need help," she screams, alarming me. "Please help us! He tried to kill us!" She uses the bar sink to wash her hands before running her eyes over me to check for blood. "There's some on your neck where he grabbed you. We'll leave that. Tell them everything that happened, swapping Danny for me in the bottle attack." I nod, glancing at the windows as blue lights shine through. "Showtime," she whispers, running for the door and busting out. I follow her lead, looking panicked and terrified. "He's up there," yells Rosey. "He killed his brother. They're on the roof."

The female police officer grabs her by the shoulders. "It's okay, you're safe now. Take a breath and tell us what happened."

"It's my fault," I sniffle. "I made her come on a date with me. The guy's a nutter."

"They started arguing, and he just stuck it right in his neck," Rosey continues. "Oh god, I think he killed him. We made a run for it and locked him on the rooftop." Police officers rush through the bar and towards the roof garden.

ARTHUR

# ARTHUR

The buzzing of my mobile across the bedside table wakes me. I grab it and head out the room, trying not to wake Jolene. "Mav?"

"Get to the club. We have a situation."

"Is Meli okay?" I ask, my heart beating faster at the thought this is to do with her.

"You might want to kill her before I do." He disconnects, and I frown. I go back into the bedroom and find Jolene's naked form still in the same position. I dress quietly and leave.

When I get to the clubhouse, I go straight to Maverick's office, where he, Grim, Rosey, Albert, and Meli are waiting. Meli is splattered in blood, and the minute she sees me, she rushes into my arms. She buries her nose against my chest, then pulls back just as quickly. "You smell of her," she murmurs, frowning.

Before I can answer, Mav stands. "Thelma and Louise here, went on a mission tonight."

"Relax," says Rosey, smirking.

Mav slams his hands on the table, and her smirk vanishes. "Don't fucking tell me to relax, Rosey. I've had it with you turning rogue on this club." She sits straighter. "You make up the rules and you don't give a crap about the rest of us."

"That's not fair," she argues. "I did this for everyone else."

# NICOLA JANE

"You just took it upon yourself," snaps Grim. "And the worst thing is, you put Meli in danger."

Meli shakes her head, pulling her hurt gaze from me as she sits back down. "I made her come with me."

"What happened?" I ask, taking the empty seat beside Meli. I don't miss the way she turns slightly away from me.

"We went on a date with the Palmer brothers," she mutters.

"Didn't you get my message?" I ask.

She shakes her head. "I didn't listen to it until after."

"What message?" asks Mav.

"Telling her not to make a date with Danny. Jolene said something about them, and it made me think she knew they were going to meet up, like it was a set-up."

"Great. So, you ignored warnings, you lied to me about when it was taking place, and you just dealt with them yourselves," Mav summarises.

"Are you okay?" I ask. "Did either of you get hurt?"

"Curtis is dead, and Danny was arrested for it," says Rosey.

"Danny killed his brother?"

"That's what we told the police," Meli says.

# ARTHUR

I pinch the bridge of my nose, giving me a second to process the information. "You spoke to the police?"

"We witnessed a murder, of course, we did," says Rosey, back to smirking again.

"Okay, start from the fucking beginning because I'm getting a headache," I growl.

"Probably the late nights," Meli mutters.

"Or maybe it's the fact I'm getting calls at five in the morning to tell me you'd got yourself into a mess," I snarl.

"Take it easy," Grim warns, and I resent the way he's protecting her. That's my job.

Mav notices and holds his hands up. "Let's all take a minute to think."

"What are we gonna tell Jolene?" mutters Albert, and we all turn our attention to him. "She'll come for us. It's the perfect excuse."

"We don't tell her," snaps Meli. "She doesn't get to know everything."

"I think she'll guess when the word gets out," Albert replies.

"You've shortened the deadline by hours," Mav adds. "It was a stupid fucking move that, as usual, wasn't thought through."

"What were we supposed to do, let them kill us?" Meli demands to know. "Because they would have if it hadn't been for Rosey."

## NICOLA JANE

"You never should have gone," I yell angrily.

Meli stands, rolling her eyes. "How dare you lecture me when you turn up here stinking of her cheap perfume!" She leaves, slamming the door. I bite my lip and clench my fists to stop me chasing her down.

"She needs sleep," Grim explains.

"And you'd know, would you?" I snap.

Grim smirks. "Apparently, better than you."

"I'm locking the club down," Mav says before I can reply. "Anyone you need to keep safe, send them here."

"Albert." I look at him, and he shrugs. He looks exhausted. "I can't do this until I know you, Tommy, and Charlie are safe. We need to find Ma before they hurt her." Albert agrees. "Did you give statements to the police?" I ask Rosey.

She shakes her head. "We've got to call into the station at ten."

I nod, standing to pace. "Okay, so what if we can somehow tie Jolene into this?" I suggest.

"I'm listening," Mav replies.

"That's it," I say. "That's all I have so far."

"What if I said something in my statement? I could say it like I don't think it's important, but when they hear it, it'll make them suspect her."

"Her husband's murder," says Albert, suddenly sitting straighter. "You were the only one on that

# ARTHUR

rooftop. You'd know details no one else could. Could you give something up that'll make them suspicious?"

Rosey nods. "Maybe. I'll have a think."

"We're still overlooking a vital part of this whole thing," says Grim. "Jolene has a price on your head, Albert, and on Meli's. That doesn't go away because she gets banged up. We still need to get that called off."

"We didn't forget, but thanks to Charlie's Angels, we've got to rethink the whole fucking plan," says Maverick, glaring at Rosey.

# Chapter Nineteen

MELI

I stir when the bed dips. Arthur gently brushes hair from my eyes and smiles. "You have to be at the police station in an hour, and Rosey needs to talk to you first."

"It's like a never-ending nightmare," I say, pushing to sit up.

"I know you're trying to help me," he says, "but please don't put yourself in danger because of it. I'll find a way to get rid of Jolene."

"What if she gets pregnant?" I ask, my voice quiet.

"I don't know," he replies, shrugging. "I hate myself right now, and I tried to end it with you so we wouldn't have to feel like this—me full of guilt and you full of hurt. But you told me to stay focussed,

# ARTHUR

didn't you?" I nod. "So, you have to do the same. She uses you as a threat constantly, and I'll do anything to keep you safe, including shit I don't want to do."

"It's just hard knowing you've . . ." I sigh heavily. "It's just hard."

He nods. "I know. The whole situation is fucked-up."

"I terminated the pregnancy with Grim," I admit.

"You don't have to tell me, Angel. I admit it pissed me off when I found out, but it was shock, that's all. You did what you had to do, and it's your past."

"It was after that I realised that I didn't hate the thought of babies as much as I thought I did. But it was too late, I'd already done it, so when Hadley told everyone she was expecting, it broke my heart. I was happy for her but so sad for myself. Then, I shut it down and told myself I was fine without kids. I'd probably only mess them up, anyway."

"Don't say that. You'll make a great mum."

"I just feel like it's going to happen all over again. Jolene's going to end up making that big announcement instead of me."

Arthur kisses me on the forehead. "It's not going to happen, Meli. I promise. Now, get up and dress. Rosey is waiting for you."

# NICOLA JANE

Rosey looks serious when I find her at the kitchen table. "Did you sleep?" I ask.

She shakes her head. "I took Ollie to school and then sat here to work out what we say to the police."

I take a seat. "Okay."

"We go with the truth. It was a date, but we were weirded out when we arrived and it was just those two in an empty bar, and when we tried to make an excuse to leave, they got nasty. But we say Curtis was aggressive. We tell them what he said about Danny attacking you and that Jolene hired them to do it because she was jealous you had a fling with Arthur."

"It's practically the truth," I say, nodding.

"Exactly. But when Curtis said all that, Danny got mad, they argued, and Danny smashed the bottle and threatened Curtis. He laughed at him, said things like he was weak and the screw-up of the family, so Danny stabbed him. We mention I went to remove the bottle in a panic, so I could help him, but you told me if I removed it, he would bleed out. That covers any DNA from me. Say Danny was acting crazed after he hurt his brother, muttering that Jo would kill him. I questioned him on that, and he told us Jolene killed her husband by pushing him off a rooftop. If they ask, we don't know who her husband was. We tell them that Danny told us she'd hired them to kill her own brothers, we say we didn't believe him and we told him that, so he told us they were placed in acid at a warehouse on Tarrant Street."

"Tarrant Street," I repeat. "Got it."

"It's important you sound natural. Pause and act like you're trying to recall details. Don't reel all this off."

I roll my eyes. "I know how to talk to the police, I've been doing it my whole life. What do I tell them about me and Arthur?"

"Just that you were sleeping together, but it ended. Don't tell them he's with Jolene, just that she likes him and he keeps giving her the brush-off."

"Won't they check on that? Her stuff is in his room."

"It won't be by the time the police get there."

"Did you find the hit person?" I smile with relief until she shakes her head.

"No, not yet, but with the club on lockdown, you'll be safe, and so will Arthur's brothers. Albert is on the way to collect their mother as we speak. Mav tracked her to Jolene's apartment."

---

The two male officers take notes while I speak. I occasionally blow my nose and wipe my eyes for effect. "I thought he was going to kill us all," I continue. "When he started talking about Jolene and how she was crazy, I really got worried. I was scared he'd call her and she'd come."

"Why did he say she was crazy?" asks one of the officers.

I shrug. "I'm not sure. He was acting terrified, saying she was going to kill him for what he'd done to his brother. Rosey laughed at him because Jolene doesn't seem the type. I mean, she's a cow, don't get me wrong, but she seems a bit dim. He said it's all an act and that she killed her husband." They both stare at me with wide eyes. "I didn't even know she had a husband cos she's been flirting with Arthur like she's single. Anyway, Danny said she killed him so . . ." I shrug.

"Did he say how she'd done that?"

I nod, wiping my eyes. "Yes, she pushed him off a rooftop. I thought they were just trying to scare us because we were up on the roof." They exchange a look, and I gasp. "Oh god, is it true?" They don't reply, instead going back to scribbling down some notes. "If she did, is it possible that . . . Danny said she . . ." I sniffle, and they both wait for me to finish. "She killed her brothers. She hired Danny and Curtis to kill them."

"Mrs. Hall's brothers were reported missing, not dead," the officer says.

"Oh good, because when he started reeling off details, I got scared."

## ARTHUR

"Details?" they repeat together.

I nod. "Yes. He said they put them in acid in a warehouse." I bite my lip like I'm thinking hard. "Tarrant Street, I think he said. Rosey just laughed at him. We thought he was just trying to scare us some more."

One of the officers closes his notepad. "Thank you, you've been very helpful."

The other officer taps his pen against his lips thoughtfully. "Just one last thing. Mr. Palmer said it was your friend who put that bottle in his brother's neck. Why would he say that?"

I frown. "We were fucking terrified," I snap. "Rosey is many things, but she's not a killer. Christ, we just went on a date and ended up in hell. I should imagine he's saying all kinds of things to get himself out of this."

The officer nods. "Okay. Thanks. We'll be in touch."

ARTHUR

I brace myself when I spot the police car pulling into the club's car park below. Albert's already been to mine to remove any trace of Jolene from my house, and he's taken it all back to her place, where he managed to get Ma and take her to the safety of the MC clubhouse.

I sit at my desk to give the illusion I'm busy, burying my head in the laptop. When the knock comes, I look up with an annoyed expression, which I immediately turn to surprise when I see the officer looking through the glass of the door. I indicate for him to come in and two officers enter. "Your manager said we could come straight up," says one.

"Of course, what can I do for you? Can I get you anything? A drink maybe?"

They shake their heads. "We'd like to speak to you regarding an incident involving Amelia—"

"Is she okay?" I ask, standing. "Is she hurt?"

One of the officers holds out his hands in a placating manner. "She's fine. Absolutely fine."

I take a deep breath, nodding and sitting back down. "Okay. Great. Good."

"What's your relationship with her?"

"Officer . . ." I wait for him to introduce himself properly.

"Apologies, Officer Patterson and Detective Inspector Stone."

"Officer Patterson, what exactly do you need to know about our relationship and why?"

"Maybe we could start by asking you about Jolene Hall," suggests Stone.

I narrow my eyes. "That woman is fast becoming a pain in my backside. I don't know her too well. I did business with her brothers, but I'm sure you know

# ARTHUR

they've been missing in action for a few weeks. Since then, she's been trying to take over their ventures. And if I'm honest, she's trying desperately hard to get into my bed."

"What business?" asks Patterson.

"They asked me to invest in a nightclub they were opening, and also a hotel. We were in talks, but then they disappeared."

"Did Mrs. Hall mention where she thought they might be?" asks Stone. "Like if they were actually missing, or if they'd gone away on holiday maybe?"

I shake my head. "She said they were missing and she'd contacted the police to report it. She asked me to sit with her when the police took a report."

"She's leaned on you since?"

I shake my head. "No. She wants to, but I don't mix business and pleasure. Well, not always." I smirk. "I did with Meli, I mean Amelia. She works for me in the office."

"Are you in a relationship?"

I shake my head. "No. Jolene thought we were, and I guess I left her to think that, hoping it would get her off my back."

"Do you know of Danny and Curtis Palmer?"

I think for a moment. "I think Jolene mentioned once or twice that they work for her. Not sure what they did exactly. Pair of thugs, from what I've heard."

"Oh, what exactly did you hear?"

I shrug. "Just rumours, Officer, nothing concrete. They're a part of the E15 gang. Actually, I also heard that Jolene took over that too."

"The E15 gang?" asks Stone.

I nod. "Apparently, though I don't know for certain. As you know, I'm clean these days." I give a smug smile. "But that's the talk of the streets."

"Would you say Jolene Hall liked you enough to try and hurt Amelia?" Stone asks.

"You said Meli was okay," I snap.

"She is."

I take a calming breath. "I guess so. She didn't like Meli and made it clear by being off with her whenever she came to the office. She would use a different name, trying to give Meli the impression she wasn't important enough to know. Just catty things, so I ignored it. Look, is Jolene in some kind of trouble? Is she the reason Meli called in sick today?"

"We suggest you speak with Amelia. If we needed you to, could you give us a statement with regards to your relationship with both women?"

I nod. "Sure."

"Great, we'll be in touch."

# ARTHUR

When I get to the MC clubhouse, I immediately go to Ma and wrap my arms around her. She laughs and tells me, "All this fuss is ridiculous."

"Are you okay?"

She nods. "They took very good care of me," she reassures me. I look over to Albert, who nods to confirm he sorted the youths who were keeping her there.

"I'm glad you're okay, Ma, and I'm so sorry."

Mama B comes over. "Your Ma is staying with us for a while. She's going to help me look after all my boys."

Ma looks happy about this, and I relax a little. "Ma loves to look after everyone," I tell her.

"You need to go and look after a certain someone," Ma whispers, nodding to the office. "She looks very tired and worried."

I smirk. "You've been digging up the gossip on me?"

"I wasn't short of women here to tell all," she says, winking.

I find Meli in Mav's office. "Have we heard anything?" asks Mav.

I shake my head. "They must have her in custody because I'm certain she'd have called by now." As I finish that sentence, my mobile rings displaying a withheld number, and I answer.

"Arthur, it's Jolene," she says.

"Why are you calling?" I snap.

"What do you mean? I need your help." She's confused by my tone, but if she's with the police or they're tapping her phone, I have to keep up the pretence that she's harassing me. "I've told you before, time and time again, we're not a thing and you have to stop calling me. Call one of your thugs."

She scoffs. "It's because of them I'm here."

"Where?"

"I've been arrested," she snaps.

"So, why are you calling me?"

"Because we're getting married," she hisses.

I laugh. "You're clearly delusional. Maybe you should ask them to check your head while you're there. This has to stop."

"Remember what I said," she growls.

"What was that?"

"You know what I'm talking about. I swear, I'll make that call."

"Um, but you've just used your one call to call me."

"Arthur, I mean it. I need a solicitor, and I need one now."

"I can't help you, I'm sorry. And please, stop calling me." I hear her cry out in frustration as I disconnect.

Rosey pops her head around the office door. "I have a lead on the hitman. I'll be back soon."

"Do you need backup?" asks Mav.

# ARTHUR

She laughs like he's making the funniest joke. "If I'm not back by morning, I want a public apology from you at my funeral, Mav. Don't forget, I love you all," she says dramatically before rushing off.

# Chapter Twenty

ROSEY

I tie my hair into a low ponytail and take a seat on the roof edge. Being on rooftops is becoming a real habit of mine. I look down at the streets below, still busy with shoppers and people going out for dinner. The fire exit that opens onto the roof swings open and a man in black appears, holding another man out in front with a gun to his head. Neither spot me, so I sit patiently, watching, waiting for the perfect time to announce my presence.

"To the edge," growls the man, shoving his prisoner hard. He stops right at the edge, his hands gripping the wall.

"Please, please, don't do this," he begs, and I roll my eyes. Don't get me wrong, I have sympathy, just

# ARTHUR

not for these kinds of men who spend their lives on the wrong side of the law and act surprised or upset when it catches up with them.

The man grabs him by the neck and hisses, "Climb on to the ledge." His prisoner carefully climbs onto the roof ledge, sobbing to himself.

"That's it?" I ask, jumping off my spot on the wall and walking towards them. The gun is immediately turned on me, and I hold my hands up. "Don't shoot, blah, blah," I say, sounding bored. "Sorry, I don't really beg."

"Who the fuck are you?" snaps the gunman.

"Rosey." I hold out my hand, and he glares at it like it's poison. I grin. "I think I have ADHD and maybe a touch of autism. I don't read social situations well, so I don't know if you want to shake hands or high five or—"

"What the fuck are you doing up here?" he snaps, waving the gun at me.

"I came to see you."

"What?" he growls, looking confused and irritated.

"You took a lot of finding, but in the end, I got there, Archer." I smile, then look at the quivering man on the ledge. "And this must be Harry Greedy. Unfortunate name."

"You're fucking with my head," snaps Archer.

"It's surprising how much I hear that." I shove Greedy, and he topples, waving his arms like he's expecting to take off in flight, and then he finally loses to gravity and falls backwards, tumbling over the edge. I lean over and watch him land with a thud. "We have minutes before he's found," I explain. "The Chinese next door usually come out to their bins around nine. I'm guessing you'd like to be gone before that happens."

"I don't know who the fuck you are or what you want but—"

"I told you, I'm Rosey. And unless you listen very carefully, you'll be caught on this roof when the police arrive."

"Fuck you," he snaps, turning back to the door. I pull out the handheld taser and press it to the back of his neck. He jolts and drops the gun, which I kick out of the way. He goes to his knees, and I grab his arms, pulling them behind his back and securing them with pull-ties.

"You're not being very nice, Archer. I came here to speak to you about my friends, and you've been very disrespectful," I tell him, moving around to his front so he can see me. "I could have killed you, you didn't even see me waiting for you, but we're in the same line of work and I figured I'd try talking first. So, can we try that?" He nods even though he looks annoyed. "Great." We hear a scream from down below. "Start the timer," I joke. "You were hired by Jolene Hall. My friends, Amelia Maverick and Albert Taylor, are on your list."

"So, if you're in this line of work, you know a job's and job. I don't get involved in the details."

"You can't go ahead now I know who you are." I slap my forehead. "Christ, you didn't even deny it. You're one of the worst hitmen out there."

"You've done your research, so what's the point in denying it?"

"Jolene Hall's been arrested. If you go ahead, you're not going to see a penny of what she owes you because I'm gonna make sure she goes down. So, you can go ahead for free and then I'll kill you, or you can walk away and call it quits."

"You're good," he mutters. "Fuck. Look, let me be straight with you, I need the cash. The jobs aren't coming in and I'm about to lose everything."

I groan. "I'm a fool for a sob story. What if I could get you work? It would take some convincing, my boss isn't good with new faces."

He nods. "Deal. I'll drop the work for Hall if you can get me some with your boss."

I go behind him and cut the binds. "We need to leave."

# Chapter Twenty-One

ARTHUR

"Rosey was like a possessed demon," Meli says, cuddling into my chest.

"She's a little unhinged," I say with a laugh. "Wonder how she got so messed-up."

"I hope her lead works out and we can put all this to an end."

I kiss her on the head. "Me too. Until then, I'm happy we can all stay under one roof."

"It must feel good to have your mum back."

I nod. "She's the glue to our family. I don't know what we'd do if she got hurt because of us."

"Did she know what you were up to when you were running in bad circles?" asks Meli.

# ARTHUR

"I think she suspected when I was handing her thousands of pounds each month to help with the bills."

She laughs. "And she wasn't worried? Did she try to stop you?"

"At first. But we needed the money, so she started to turn a blind eye. I hate she worked her backside off to provide for her kids and still couldn't quite feed us properly. It's crazy people struggle like that in this day and age. That's why I employ mainly women in my factories and hotels. Most of them are single mothers who just need a decent wage and an understanding boss."

She arches a brow and glances up at me. "Understanding?"

I grin. "I am. They get paid leave, emergency days for childcare issues, bonuses . . . I'm a good boss."

She kisses me. "Good to know."

I push her onto her back. "Which reminds me, you promised me kids," I say, laying over her. She cups my face in her hands, but her expression tells me I'm not going to like what she's about to say.

"I love you, Arthur Taylor, and what I said stands. But I'm having a hard time with the whole you and Jolene thing. I know you did it to protect everyone, but it still hurts."

I flop down beside her and nod. "I get it. Take your time."

The door opens and Rosey barges in. "Mav wants us in his office so I can update you."

"Did you get him?" I ask.

She grins. "Have I ever let you down yet?"

We step into the office to find a man already sitting down opposite Maverick. "This is Archer," says Rosey with a smile.

"The hitman," Mav clarifies, shaking his head in exasperation.

"Now, before you all start fussing, let me just say, he's agreed not to take the hit," Rosey announces. She claps her hands and smiles in delight. "Great news, right?"

"So, why is he here?" asks Grim.

"I was getting to that part," she replies. "Arthur, meet your new... erm... me. He's going to replace me."

"Sorry?" I ask, not because I didn't hear her but because I need her to repeat the words again, so I know she's serious.

"He needs money, and I need a break."

"Who takes a fucking career break from killing?" snaps Grim.

"It's hard work," Rosey argues, "and I want to spend time with Ollie."

"Like parental leave?" asks Meli, smirking at our recent conversation.

"Exactly," says Rosey.

# ARTHUR

"I don't know this guy," I point out.

"Which is why I'll be here to help advise him," Rosey says. "Look, he's agreed to drop the hit for work. He needs money, and we need Meli and Albert to live so . . ."

I sigh. "We'll talk about it further. I'll take your number and call for a meeting tomorrow."

Archer grins. "Great. Thanks, Mr. Taylor." We shake hands, and Rosey shows him out. I'll have to do background checks and then find something I can use against him to keep him loyal.

"Just when I think she can't get weirder," mutters Maverick.

# Epilogue

*Three months later...*

MELI

I watch Rylee rubbing her hand over her large pregnant stomach. Arthur comes up behind me and wraps his arms around me. "I love you," he whispers.

"I love you too," I reply, smiling.

"I think we could sneak away," he adds.

I laugh. "It's Astraea and Rylee's baby shower. I didn't go to all the trouble of organising such a fabulous party to miss it."

"If you keep brushing me off, you'll never be having a baby shower yourself," he complains.

I turn in his arms and kiss him. "I seem to remember trying a lot for our own baby," I remind him. "Just this morning being one of those times."

# ARTHUR

"It seems a long time ago."

"I'm going to enjoy the rest of the afternoon, and then I'll pack for our flight," I say, kissing him.

Jolene was in court this morning for her sentencing. She was found guilty of murdering her husband as well as conspiring to murder her brothers and was sentenced to life imprisonment with no parole. Danny is still awaiting sentencing for the murders of Curtis, Leon, and Max, but it's expected he'll be sentenced to life in prison as well. It felt like a relief, and when Arthur announced a break away for us both, I jumped at the chance. A man's never taken me on holiday, not one that Mav could trust.

I wait until Rylee and Astraea have cut their cakes before I sneak upstairs to pack. Hadley comes in and sits on the bed. "Are you excited?"

I nod. "He hasn't told me where we're going."

"I'm sure it'll be perfect. You look really happy, Meli."

I smile. "I am."

"Good. It's about time." She hugs me. "I love you."

"I love you too."

"It's so nice to see you smile. For once, it looks genuine."

She leaves me to pack, and I think over her words. She's right. For the first time in my life, I am happy, and I mean those words. They're not forced or used to hide my sadness. Arthur Taylor makes me happy.

# NICOLA JANE

Arthur's driver stops the car right on the tarmac by a small plane. I laugh, looking out the car window like a child. "A private plane?" I screech.

"Of course," says Arthur, getting out the car and coming around to my side to open the door for me. He takes my hands and leans in for a kiss before leading me towards the plane.

We climb the steps and we're greeted warmly by the air hostess who shows us into the plane. We're seated in large, comfy chairs and given champagne. "I didn't take you for the romantic type," I say, sipping my drink.

"You deserve it after everything you've been through. If it wasn't for me, you wouldn't have gotten involved in anything to do with Jolene."

"We've been over this," I tell him.

"I know, but this is my way of trying to make up for it. I'll never put you in danger again."

"Some things are out of your control, Arthur."

"Have you thought about my offer?" he asks.

I nod. Arthur asked me to move in with him when we get home. "I'd love to."

"Really?"

"It'll be weird not being at the clubhouse and surrounded by everyone, but I think it'll work."

# ARTHUR

He pulls out his iPad. "Which is why I brought this." He holds it out for me to take, and I stare at the picture of some land. "It's behind the MC. Planning permission is just going through. I thought we could build our own place where you'll still be near everyone."

I stare at him in disbelief. "You'd do that for me?"

He nods. "I have a feeling Rylee will be needing you around, and Ma wants to stay at the clubhouse to help Mama B. They've really hit it off."

I throw myself at him, and he wraps me in his arms. "I love you so much," I whisper.

"I love you too, Angel. And for the record, this is not a free pass for Rosey to be around all the time." I laugh, knowing full well I'll never get rid of Rosey if I'm just a few steps away.

---

We land in Paris. I've never been, and it doesn't escape my attention that I once mentioned this to him when he asked me about ideal dates. "I hope you don't mind, but we have to get to dinner," he tells me, opening the door to the waiting car.

We're driven to the Eiffel Tower, and I clutch my hands to my chest. "You're taking me on my ideal date," I whisper.

"We've been seeing each other for a while and I've never taken you on a real date," he replies, helping me out the car.

We take the elevator to the top of the tower, where the restaurant overlooks Paris. "It's a taster menu," the waiter tells us as we're seated.

"We'll take the seven courses and a bottle of red," Arthur orders.

"Have you been here before?" I ask.

"They do business breakfast here, and it's a good way to seal a deal. But if you're asking if I've been on a date here, no. I don't date. I told you how the last relationship ended. I'm just not good at them."

"Well, as long as I walk away alive, I'll consider this to be a good date," I reply, smirking.

"Have you dated like this?"

I laugh, looking around at the extravagant restaurant. "No. The most I got out of a date was fish and chips by the docks."

"Then we'll both have made a good first memory."

Our food arrives, and as I tuck into the delicate crab meat, I groan in pleasure. "This is amazing."

"You keep making those noises and we're not finishing dinner," he growls. By the seventh course, I'm practically orgasming over the food.

"I can't eat another thing."

"We should walk it off," he tells me before asking to settle the bill.

# ARTHUR

We step out into the cool fresh air, and Arthur spins me to face him. "I have one more thing to do before I take you to a very exclusive hotel with large four-poster beds and silk sheets just like you requested." I kiss him, thinking nothing he could do can top dinner. "I love you. I love you more than I've ever loved anyone. You make me into this nice guy who takes you on dates in Paris when I should be working. I like being that guy, and with you, I think that's possible." He drops onto one knee, and I gasp. People around slow to watch as he pulls out a small box. "Amelia Maverick, will you marry me?"

"Arthur," I whisper, "everyone's looking."

"You better give me an answer then," he says, adding a nervous laugh.

"Yes! Yes, of course, I will!"

He lets out a breath, standing, then he takes the ring from the box and places it onto my finger, where the large, round diamond sparkles. I wrap my arms around his neck, and he spins me around. Spectators clap before moving along. After a few minutes, Arthur lowers me to the ground.

"I love you too," I tell him. "I never thought I'd find anyone to love me, for me, and you do, you really do. I didn't know happiness before you, Arthur, and right now, I'm so happy, my heart could burst."

He kisses me. "You're perfect, Angel, just the way you are." He takes me by the hand. "Now, let's go make that family you promised me."

# A Note from me to you

MANY OF YOU WERE waiting for Meli's story and it was a shock when I revealed Arthur was her love interest. I didn't get much say in the matter, these books often have a mind of their own. My original plan was for Rosey and Arthur, but they just didn't gel together.

Next up will be Albert's story. So look out for more details in my readers group on Facebook.

If you enjoyed Arthur, please share the love. Tell everyone, by leaving a review or rating on Amazon, Goodreads, or wherever else you find it. You can also follow me on social media. I'm literally everywhere, but here's my linktr.ee to make it easier. https://linktr.ee/NicolaJaneUK

# NICOLA JANE

I'm a UK author, based in Nottinghamshire. I live with my husband of many years, our two teenage boys and our four little dogs. I write MC and Mafia romance with plenty of drama and chaos. I also love to read similar books. Before I became a full-time author, I was a teaching assistant working in a primary school.

If you'd like to follow my writing journey, join my readers group on Facebook, the link is above. You can also use that link if you're a book blogger, I'd love you to sign up to my team.

# Popular books by Nicola Jane

### **The Kings Reapers MC**

Riggs' Ruin https://mybook.to/RiggsRuin
Capturing Cree https://mybook.to/CapturingCree
Wrapped in Chains https://mybook.to/WrappedinChains
Saving Blu https://mybook.to/SavingBlu
Riggs' Saviour https://mybook.to/RiggsSaviour
Taming Blade https://mybook.to/TamingBlade
Misleading Lake https://mybook.to/MisleadingLake
Surviving Storm https://mybook.to/SurvivingStorm

NICOLA JANE

Ravens Place https://mybook.to/RavensPlace
Playing Vinn https://mybook.to/PlayingVinn

### The Perished Riders MC

Maverick https://mybook.to/Maverick-Perished
Scar https://mybook.to/Scar-Perished
Grim https://mybook.to/Grim-Perished
Ghost https://mybook.to/GhostBk4
Dice https://mybook.to/DiceBk5

### The Hammers MC (Splintered Hearts Series)

Cooper https://mybook.to/CooperSHS
Kain https://mybook.to/Kain
Tanner https://mybook.to/TannerSH

Printed in Dunstable, United Kingdom